If he kissed her again, every sensible thought she possessed would flee.

'Colby.' His name was spoken on a ragged breath.

'It's not fair,' he said in a voice that sounded rougher.

Was it possible that she'd made him feel as if the earth had rocked? That's how she'd felt. 'What isn't?'

Feather light, he kissed one corner and then the other of her mouth. 'How wonderful you taste.'

'I have to go inside.' She gestured over her shoulder.

'Why?'

A quiet challenge stretched between them. 'Because I don't know what I want,' Tessa said honestly.

With reluctance, he released her. Before she turned, he touched her chin, forced her eyes to meet his. 'I do,' he whispered. 'I want you.'

Available in June 2003 from Silhouette Special Edition

Big Sky Cowboy
JENNIFER MIKELS

SILHOUETTE®
SPECIAL EDITION™

Silhouette, Silhouette Special Edition and Colophon are registered trademarks of Harlequin Books S.A., used under licence.

First published in Great Britain 2003
Silhouette Books, Eton House, 18-24 Paradise Road,
Richmond, Surrey TW9 1SR

© Harlequin Books S.A. 2002

Special thanks and acknowledgement are given to Jennifer Mikels for her contribution to the Montana series.

ISBN 0 373 24491 6

23-0603

Printed and bound in Spain
by Litografia Rosés S.A., Barcelona

For Karen Taylor Richman.
Thank you again.

JENNIFER MIKELS

is from Chicago, Illinois, but now resides in Phoenix, Arizona, with her husband, two sons and a shepherd-collie. She enjoys reading, sports, antiques, car-boot sales and long walks. Though she's done technical writing in public relations, she loves writing romantic fiction and happy endings.

Prologue

Centuries ago she'd have been called a witch. Colby Holmes remained undecided about Tessa Madison's psychic abilities or if she was loony or not, but she didn't look the way he'd imagined—a bohemian type with frizzy hair, too much makeup, too many bracelets and beads. No, that wasn't how she looked at all.

"Man, it's hot, ain't it, Colby?"

With effort he dragged his gaze away from the raven-haired woman and nodded at the teenager, a sixteen-year-old who loved rodeo and often displayed a hint of hero worship. "Real hot."

Heat, a sultry warmth that belonged in the tropics instead of Big Sky country, had made Montana temperatures soar. The unseasonably warm July air carried no breeze. Even while he stood still, doing nothing, sweat dampened the back of his shirt.

Yet she looked cool. So damn cool, Colby mused. She wore some gauzy-looking, pale blue dress that skirted her ankles. He eyed the sandaled heels, the toenails painted a frosty-looking pink color. The sheen on her bare arms.

Petite, she had an easy stride that slightly swayed the subtle curve of her hips. Shiny black hair curtained an oval-shaped face as if protecting the fairness of her skin. She appeared fragile—delicate features, small hands, slim body.

He'd heard she lived alone, had no relatives near. Independent, he assumed. And he'd heard talk. Some people wanted her gone from town. But here she was. He admired people who knew how to hang tough.

He'd been told she was twenty-four, had moved to town two months ago. She'd opened her store in a Victorian that was painted a crisp white with dark green trim and shutters. Called Mystic Treasures, it was right around the corner from Main Street and other businesses. It catered to people who were lured to the mystical world of palmistry and astrological readings and believed in extrasensory perception and premonitions.

Colby braced a shoulder against an upright near the arched, flowered trellis the bride and groom had stood beneath moments ago. Along with moonlight, the malibu lights strung along the back of the ranch house fell on the guests gathering around Sylvia and Larry Hardy.

For another moment, Colby watched Tessa Madison inch her way around the buffet table, which was draped with a white linen tablecloth and filled with serving dishes. He gave no conscious thought to his actions. When he moved near to reach for a plate from the stack, she faced him. Her delicate fingers cradled a piece of bacon wrapped around something green. With her other hand, she reached for the plate, handed it to him. "Do you want one?"

Instead of taking the plate right away, he stared at her hand, thin-fingered, the nails tipped with clear polish. "Thanks." It was dumb, but he wanted to stare at her eyes. Haunting eyes. Gray, fringed by long, dark lashes, they held a smile as they met his. "I'm Colby Holmes."

Her smile widened. "I know," she announced in a tone that conveyed he hadn't needed to tell her.

She knows? Colby watched her turn away, stroll across the grass. *What does that mean? Nothing. It's nothing.*

"Colby." At the sound of his father's voice, he swung around. Strands of gray weaved through brown hair the same color as Colby's. More than once, Colby had been told that he looked like his father when Bud Holmes had been younger, trimmer. "Are you listening to me?"

"No, I didn't catch what you said, Dad." *I was drooling over the town's resident eccentric.*

"So will you bring the car around?"

"Right." He began working his way toward the cars.

"The heat wilted the bridal bouquet," a woman

standing near the flowered trellis complained to another woman.

"Tessa told Sylvia to have silk flowers," her companion responded. "But Sylvia's cousin works at the florist's and would have boycotted the wedding if Sylvia hadn't ordered flowers from her."

"I listened to Tessa when she told me to see my sister in Oregon. It's good that I did. She went into labor five minutes after I arrived."

Colby frowned. He'd reached a point where he'd try anything to get normalcy back into his family's lives. No one was getting answers about his aunt's murder. When Chelsea Kearns, the forensic expert in town, had suggested he take a less traditional route and talk to the woman only a handful of people had known was psychic, he'd reluctantly considered the notion.

Since then, Tessa Madison's so-called powers had become the talk of the town. According to people who believed in clairvoyants, she could help him.

He gave himself a mental kick. He must be nuts to think about going to see her. He didn't believe she had any supernatural power. No one could see what wasn't visible.

Chapter One

"He's coming in."

The he was Colby Holmes. Tessa swung a look away from her store assistant to the man at the shop entrance. She'd had a premonition about him, one she'd wanted to ignore. She let her gaze move up long legs encased in snug, worn-looking jeans. Briefly she glanced at the ornate rodeo buckle, took in the broad shoulders in the blue chambray shirt, the well-defined muscles in sinewy arms beneath the rolled-up sleeves. An ex-rodeo champion who fluttered the hearts of most women under the age of forty, he tipped back his square-crowned, beige Stetson.

She studied the strong face with the high cheekbones, the sharply drawn jaw. In his late twenties, lean of hip, rugged-looking, he bore a few lines at the corners of brown eyes. A summer tan emphasized just how dark those deep-set eyes were.

"He's so sexy," Marla said under her breath. Single, in her late twenties, with straw-colored blond hair that hung to her mid back, Marla was a born romantic, convinced love was just around the corner despite a breakup a week ago from her childhood sweetheart. Freethinking, she possessed the right mind-set for working at the shop with its New Age merchandise. She'd become indispensable to Tessa. More important, in two months, she'd become a loyal friend.

Marla wandered over to her twin sister, Regina, who'd come in for a numerology book. The only other customer was octogenarian Margaret Hansen.

Tessa laid a deck of tarot cards on the display counter. The top card was the Queen of Cups. Tessa groaned. It usually signified romance. Well, she had expected him, hadn't she? The moment his fingers had brushed hers when she'd handed him the plate yesterday, she'd felt the warning jolt and a quick breathless sensation. But premonitions weren't written in stone. She'd stay clear of him and block any future contact.

Prepared, she looked up. She knew what he wanted, and she didn't want any part of it. He didn't look too friendly, she decided. In the newspaper, he'd always worn a wide smile, the smile of a champion. At the moment, he bore a less than congenial expression, his mouth set in a tight line. Well-schooled at masking her uneasiness behind a breezy demeanor, she flashed a bright smile. "Hi, again. Did you enjoy the wedding?"

"Did you?" He stopped beside a table where she'd set out a Ouija board.

"Yes, I did. Sylvia's a friend." Except for Marla, her twin sister, Regina, and several customers, Sylvia was one of the few friends Tessa had made since arriving in town. "There was such a positive karma there." His frown deepened, as she'd hoped it would. She needed to discourage him quickly.

"Was there?"

"Yes, but your aura is disturbing." For extra effect, she wrinkled her nose. "Greenish. You should come in for a psychic reading."

"I'll pass."

Of course, he would. This was not a whimsical man. "Oh, you're not of that mind."

For a moment he said nothing. He didn't need to. His eyes narrowed, and he looked at her as if she was crazy. "No, I'm not."

"Too bad. You definitely need to cleanse your subconscious of cosmic disturbances. If you change your mind come see me." Before he could respond, she turned away. Skirting the counter, she resisted an urge to roll a shoulder against the tension bunching her muscles. On more than one occasion, she'd dissuaded a man with a glimpse of Tessa, the space cadet.

Since Chelsea Kearns had revealed Tessa's psychic power, she had been backpedaling, trying to keep a low profile. Tessa wanted so badly to stay in Rumor, to be a part of the community. Different scared some people. Like Leone Burton, she mused. A member of the town council, a pillar of society, the woman was influential, and she didn't like Tessa.

Earlier, Leone had stormed in. Gray-haired with ramrod-straight posture, she'd declared war on Tessa's store. She'd see Tessa gone from town, she said. She wouldn't allow some fortune-teller to play parlor games with the good people of Rumor.

Tessa wished she could go back to bed, start the day over. She entered the storeroom, paused beside crates of unopened merchandise and reached for the crowbar on top of the worn-looking oak desk.

In the doorway, Regina, still holding the book on numerology she'd been thumbing through, peered at her. "He wants your help, Tessa."

Tessa pried at one of the metal clips that clamped the top of a crate. "Are you going to the antiques sale tonight, Regina?" she asked instead of responding.

Marla suddenly appeared. "You should help him. Everyone likes him, Tessa."

Regina was just as eager to play Colby Holmes's advocate. "Tell her more about him," she urged. "You want to know, don't you, Tessa?"

"He used the rodeo winnings he'd saved over years to buy a small ranch and trains horses now. Quarter horses."

They were wrong. She didn't want to know too much about him. She'd felt more than a connection with his nearness. Sensation had swarmed in on her. She'd dodged it then, planned to keep it at bay. That was sensible. Though he might view her as foolish with an absurd lifestyle, Tessa weighed situations, always considered the consequences of her actions. Avoiding him and his problem was the right decision.

"Tessa, he's coming back here," Marla said in an excited whisper with a glance over her shoulder.

Tessa straightened to see him standing in the doorway. Flattening a palm against the doorjamb, he looked as if he planned to stay there. "We need to talk."

She never expected him to be so obstinate. "I told you—"

He stepped around Marla and bridged the distance in a few strides. "I know what you said."

Head bent, Tessa yanked at the lid on one crate. She stared at the dusty toes of his boots when he stopped inches from her. With the crowbar, she fiercely yanked at the metal clips that clamped the top of a crate.

"Give me that," he said, closing a hand over the crowbar.

Her hand wasn't quite steady. She looked up, saw that Marla and Regina had disappeared, left her alone with him. "A reflexologist would help you. I sense you're tense." Actually she was the tense one.

With more force than necessary, he worked at the lid, then flipped the final clip on the crate. "My state of mind isn't why I'm here."

"Are you looking for something in particular?" Perhaps he wouldn't ask her to help if she treated him as a customer, if he thought her too odd. "If you want a reading, I can do your astrological chart. You're a Taurus. Stubborn, steadfast, persistent.''

His frown deepening, he set the crowbar on an adjacent crate. ''A Taurus? How do you know what…''

''You were born in May. So that's your birth sign. It's the bull,'' she said and stepped out of the storeroom. She waited until he stood beside her, then gestured toward palm-size crystals in various colors displayed in the store window. ''Or we have several healing crystals, if that's what you're looking for.''

As she'd expected, he stared at her again as if she was short a full deck. ''Healing crystals?''

''They'll help when your shoulder aches.''

''When my—'' His dark eyes slitted. ''Is that knowledge about my shoulder supposed to impress me?'' She didn't miss the cynicism lacing his voice. ''Everyone knows I had a dislocated shoulder.''

Tessa was accustomed to mistrust, but for some reason, she wanted to prove to him she wasn't a liar or a fake. ''Yes, that's true.'' The act wasn't working. He wouldn't go away no matter how difficult she seemed to be. Tessa went with the truth, hoping it might throw him off guard, confuse him even more. ''Like me, they probably read all of that about you in the newspaper.''

A hint of an amused smile tugged up the corners of his mouth.

She'd heard he was well-liked. In fact, she couldn't recall anyone saying anything uncomplimentary about him.

''You're a bit of a local hero, Mr. Holmes. One

newspaper article was a biographical piece.'' She knew more. People talked about him. Responsible. Practical. He was so sensible he'd retired from rodeo. Another man might have foolishly kept competing even though an injury had made him less capable. He was generous with his time and money. He would come to a friend's or neighbor's aid without being asked. But socially he'd become a loner since a broken engagement to a young woman from a neighboring Montana town.

He moved closer to a counter. A fan on it fluttered sun-streaked strands of his brown hair away from his forehead. ''What's this for?'' he asked, drawing her away from her thoughts.

She pivoted to see him gesturing at the display of scented candles. She couldn't resist a tease at his expense. ''Light.''

Straight, dark brows bunched with his scowl.

''Some people buy them for romance,'' she said to lighten the moment.

''Or séances?''

Tessa went on. ''Other people find tarot cards and Ouija boards and dowsing rods interesting.''

''All things to help tell the future.''

''If that's what a customer wants. I don't use crystal balls or tea leaves or tarot cards.''

''I heard differently. I heard you can read crystals to predict the future. Something about different crystals meaning different things.''

Why would he have bothered to learn about that?

"Crystal clairvoyants cast five crystals. The pattern in which they fall tells the future."

"But you don't do that?" He stopped beside shelves where she'd displayed ginger jars containing herbs, decks of tarot cards, astrological charts and the colored crystals.

"I can, but I don't predict."

He pivoted toward another wall of shelves displaying tea leaf cups, runes, Celtic crosses and candles. "You told Sylvia not to have real flowers."

She couldn't help smiling. "Yes, I did."

He kept staring at the high ceiling as if something important was written on it. Hanging from a beam, a giant brilliant blue sphere rotated in slow motion in a corner of the room. "Isn't that predicting?"

"I never told her they would wilt."

"This building must be a devil to keep cool," he said suddenly.

Tessa nearly laughed at the so serious, practical observation. "Not usually." The cost of heating or cooling the old building had seemed inconsequential to her. She'd fallen in love with the Victorian. It had carried a positive aura with its warm, homey feel. At the time, she'd needed to keep negativity out of her life. She doubted this man would understand such whimsical thinking. "It has been miserably hot," she finally added.

"Global warming." A crackly voice cut in. Tessa smiled at Margaret Hansen, one of her best customers but a legendary eavesdropper. The elderly lady had a penchant for hot-pink fingernail polish. Today it matched the artificial pink rose stuck in her snow-white hair. "Can I see that one?" she asked, pointing to an astrological chart under a glass display.

The store occupied the first floor of the Victorian. Tessa had replaced one of the side windows with a huge, octagonal-shaped one. On sunny days, light poured into the room. Italian lights outlined display shelves. In the middle of the room near the checkout counter was a black wrought-iron spiral staircase that led to a loft and shelves of books about astral projection, channeling, I Ching, even herb cooking.

She withdrew the astrological chart for Margaret. "Look it over, Mrs. Hansen. See if it's what you want." Tessa crossed to Colby. He was staring at the storeroom. "Yes, it was once a kitchen. Still is, but I cook upstairs in my apartment."

He slanted a look at her. "Is supplying an answer before I ask a question supposed to be a demonstration of your mind reading ability?"

"It's called observation. I saw you looking back there. Why are you here?"

"Don't you know why?"

"Yes, I've heard." Tessa had read the newspaper stories about Harriet Martel's murder. Colby's aunt had been forty-three, the head librarian and four months pregnant.

As if tempted, he touched the deck of red tarot cards. "My aunt—"

"Was Harriet Martel," she finished for him. "I've heard about her. I'm very sorry."

He was going to ask her. She knew there was no

other reason for him to have stepped into her store. Too practical. This was a logical, realistic man who believed in only what he could see.

"I want to hire you." Often people, even those who viewed her as a fraud, considered asking for her help when all else failed. "The sheriff's investigation is at a dead end." He honestly sounded stymied.

Tessa rushed a refusal before he explained more. "I'm sorry for your loss, but I can't get involved."

He drilled a look at her that carried both annoyance and puzzlement. "I understand you know my mother, Louise Holmes."

She wasn't a fool. He was leading her in a different direction deliberately. "Yes." Her guard went up with his shift in conversation. "Louise is a lovely woman." A friend of Sylvia's, Louise had come into the store several times during the past two weeks. Tessa had seen a photograph of Harriet and had noted a resemblance between her and Louise Holmes. Louise was softer-looking, and unlike the unsmiling Harriet, Louise possessed one of the most wonderful smiles Tessa had ever seen. A hundred-watt, sunshiny smile that conveyed warmth and genuine friendliness. Tessa had yet to see Colby really smile, couldn't help wondering if he had the same smile.

She'd met his father, too. Handsome, he was an older, heavier version of Colby. Known as Bud since his days as star quarterback at the local high school, Adam Holmes had been a rancher all his life. He and Louise were well-liked by a lot of people in town.

"It was bad enough when my mother thought Harriet had died by her own hand, when everyone, including Sheriff Reingard, thought she'd committed suicide.''

"They know now it was murder.''

"Right. When my mother learned Harriet had been killed, she was stunned.''

Tessa wanted to turn away, but she heard such affection in his voice when he talked about his mother.

"She won't rest unless we find out who killed Harriet.''

Nice, Tessa thought. Mr. Macho, Mr. Rugged was nice—sensitive. In seconds, she'd learned he was a good son. He'd unveiled a wealth of family concern. She'd known another man who'd never understood loyalty to family, who could ignore responsibilities without a glance back.

"Look, I wasn't as close to her as I'd been when younger. She'd been living in Boston for a while, and when she came back to Rumor, I was on the rodeo circuit.''

And he felt guilty for not being around for her.

"I've heard she was unhappy, especially during the past few months.''

That Harriet was having an affair had fueled the gossip.

"You've probably heard. The sheriff's investigation is stalled. For a while, everyone was convinced the killer was local. Now we're not so sure because of Warren Parrish.'' Anger teetered just below the surface of his voice. "He claims he's Harriet's estranged husband. One day weeks ago he unexpectedly arrived in town."

In spite of herself, curiosity got the best of her. "Do you think he killed her?"

"I don't like him. I wouldn't mind seeing him gone and behind bars. There was a book in Harriet's house with blood on it. Her own. She used it to print some letters. H and I and an N or M or R. I'll see if I can get the book for you."

Tessa shook her head. "I don't want it, Mr. Holmes."

"Colby. Call me Colby. Chelsea Kearns, the forensic expert, has come up with a profile of the killer. I'll get it for you and—"

"You're not listening. I'm sorry, but I can't help."

"A lot of people believe that you can," he quipped.

She refused to let him bait her. She wanted him to leave—now. He was more than she'd bargained for. And what she was feeling went far beyond his great looks. With a look, a moment's insight into his sensitivity, she felt her pulse rate accelerate. No one had unbalanced her so quickly, so easily before. "That's their problem, not mine," she said, watching his gaze shift from her eyes to her lips. She couldn't let herself connect with him. "You'll have to find help elsewhere." Before he could say more, she stepped away to check a delivery sheet.

When she heard his footsteps, knew he was moving away, she breathed easier. He was asking too much of her. She couldn't afford to draw attention to her psychic power if she wanted to make a home in Rumor. Too many years of moving around, she assumed, made her want to stay. She wanted to feel as if she belonged somewhere. And she could lose her chance to have that because of him, because of what he wanted from her.

Colby mumbled to himself during the drive home. One look at her eyes had almost made a believer out of him. Gray, disturbing, they seemed to see inside him. Could she read minds? How in the devil had she known he was thinking about the storeroom having once been the kitchen?

He gave his head a mental shake as he passed under the arched Double H at the entrance of the ranch. The mistake was that he'd taken a lengthy view of her in the snug jeans and bright yellow T-shirt. She hadn't looked like a kook.

He braked near the stable and climbed out of the truck. Standing on the dirt drive, he shaded eyes against a bright sun. Wide-open rangeland blended with distant buttes. He scanned the corral, the bunkhouse and stables. This was a world he understood. This was where he belonged.

He shouldn't have gone to her store. Blame it on the heat, he mused. It had been so hot lately. He wasn't thinking any more clearly than anyone else right now.

In the barn, hay crunched beneath the soles of his boots while he moved past horse stalls, then grabbed a pitchfork. Second sight. No one had it. What she really was was a modern-day Gypsy of sorts with her fortune-telling and astrological readings.

When she'd spieled off the mumbo jumbo about karma and psychic readings, he'd thought Chelsea had gotten the wrong impression of her. But he wasn't a dumb man. It hadn't taken long to guess she'd been acting the nutcase for his benefit. Later, she'd given herself away. Instead of giving him some cunning nonsense about her power allowing her to know his birth sign, she'd surprised him and offered a logical answer. She'd read a newspaper article about him, she'd said.

He poked the pitchfork hard, harder than necessary, into the bed of hay. He rarely lied to himself and couldn't now. His foul mood had more to do with what hadn't happened. For a brief moment, right before he'd left, he'd gotten lost in those eyes and had nearly drawn her close just to see her reaction. It had been a while since he'd been with a woman, he reminded himself. If he'd felt a heat curling in his gut, blame it on that.

Annoyed with what he viewed as stupid daydreaming, he worked longer than he'd intended. By the time he finished the chore, he needed a shower. Simpler surroundings suited him. He was a man who spent most of the daylight hours outside. His ranch required constant attention.

Colby shook his head with annoyance. He had things to do and lately he'd been distracted from the ranch, in town more than at home. He'd chosen to raise quarter horses. One had faithfully helped him earn plenty of money. They were the cream of rodeo horses, perfect as reining and cutting horses. He'd already had a rancher in Wyoming and a dude ranch owner in Colorado contact him because the horses were great on the trail, and some fellow from England had called him about purchasing a few for hunts.

In passing, he patted the rump of the prize mare he'd purchased less than three months ago. He'd been taken with her. Because she was no cow pony, he spent more than made sense for her, but she was a fair beauty, pale beige with a white mane and tail, had a hint of thoroughbred. She stood proud. She'd bear champions. But she still wasn't pregnant.

He lifted off his hat and used the back of his hand to wipe away sweat as he strolled toward the barn door. He stepped outside into the almost stifling heat. Hotter than hell. A setting sun peeked below the gathering pewter-gray clouds and bathed everything in a warm golden glow, made the air sticky with the promise of rain.

With thoughts about a shower, he passed the outdoor ring where one of his ranch hands was reining a horse sharply around a barrel. Hooves spraying a cloud of dirt into the air, the horse circled the first barrel tightly and then hurtled toward a second at the other end of the ring. She'd be ready for sale soon.

He'd barely stepped inside the house and removed his hat when his cell phone rang. He tossed his hat on a table in the front hall and unhooked the phone from his belt. Only a few people had the number. His mother was one of them.

"Colby, we're still waiting."

The greeting made him laugh. "Hello, Mom."

"Did you find our future daughter-in-law today?"

He indulged her. "Should I have?"

"We'd hoped," she said with a lightness that assured him this was as much a game as a serious discussion.

"Yeah, I know."

"You say that, but I don't think you take your father and me seriously." Her voice carried humor. "You need to get married. We're waiting for our grandchild."

Here it comes, Colby mused. Once a week, his mother gave her we-won't-live-forever lecture.

"We need an heir, Colby."

It was useless to tell her not to plan a wedding. While she had high hopes, he'd given them up. There was no perfect woman for him. Diana Lynscot had ended his belief in the forever-after daydream, and he wasn't sure he wanted to bother looking for another woman.

"Colby, are you listening?"

"To every word, Mom."

Some of the humor left her voice. "What about our other problem? Did you see Tessa today?"

"I talked to her. She's not interested."

Disappointment filled her voice. "Oh."

"Have you ever been in that shop?"

"Of course."

"It's unusual," he said. The store hadn't been what he'd expected. He'd been envisioning black walls, witches' spells and vampire lore. Instead he'd seen unicorns and charms for good luck.

"That's what makes it so interesting," she said without hesitation. She had such a great capacity for accepting people and anything new.

"She's unusual," he said.

"I think she's lovely. Don't you?"

A mild description. Tessa Madison was something else. Cool on the surface. Smiling even when provoked. Controlled. He admired that. He'd followed her movement around the store. He liked the way she moved. It was that simple. "Mom, we'll get answers."

"I want people to understand what a wonderful person Harriet was. There's been so much gossip."

And that hurt her, Colby knew.

"Harriet wasn't difficult or peevish. She was a strong-minded, independent woman. A woman with many fine qualities. She wasn't always easy to understand. But she was special and caring around your father and me. You need to let Tessa help," she said more firmly.

"There are other ways."

"Colby, don't be difficult."

He wasn't the one being difficult. "I asked her, Mom. She's really not interested."

"Sweetheart, please try again. I know she can help. You will, won't you?"

He thought he'd be wasting time, but offered her another assurance before saying goodbye. When his aunt had died, he'd felt useless. Well, this wasn't about him. It was about his mother, about her love, her memories of her sister.

He withdrew a business card he'd plucked up at Mystic Treasures and dialed the phone number. "Tessa Madison," he requested of Marla, Tessa's employee.

"Tessa isn't here."

"This is Colby Holmes."

An excited edge crept into her voice. "She's not here. She went to the antiques sale."

"Thanks." Colby set down the receiver. He needed to get this problem handled—now. He cursed the situation. The last thing he wanted to do was walk around the town square and look for the Gypsy lady.

Chapter Two

It was so blessed hot even at dusk. Colby scanned the sea of faces as people browsed from table to table, looking at clocks and crystal and antique jewelry. He stopped beside a table displaying Civil War guns. How hard could it be to find someone who looked like her? She was hardly ordinary with all that black hair and that trim little body.

"A good showing, huh, Colby?"

Colby let Tessa's image drift away and forced himself to face the ex-mayor, a fiftyish, barrel-chested man with a receding hairline and a reputation as a ladies' man since his divorce five years ago.

"It was a good idea to have this at night instead of the day. Don't you think?"

Colby knew he was looking for a pat on the back.

"I heard you suggested that to Pierce," he said, referring to the town's present mayor. "Real smart idea, Henry."

Henry nodded thanks, then gestured in the direction of the tall, ruddy-faced man whose dark blond hair was threaded with gray. "Stay away from the sheriff," he said about Dave Reingard. "He's sure been in a foul mood for days."

"It's the heat," Colby said. "Everyone's grumpy." But who could blame Dave? Colby mused. He had a murder to solve and a lot of pressure to do it quickly. Colby noticed that the deputy sheriff, Holt Tanner, stood near Dave. Colby doubted either man had an eye for the old furniture. They'd shown up at the antiques fair because people were tense, needed to see law enforcement was nearby.

"We need to find the killer," he heard one woman say to her husband.

"We could all be killed in our beds," an elderly man commented to a friend.

Concern had increased that a killer was lurking. Colby figured nothing would alleviate that worry except the sheriff announcing he'd arrested someone. Warren Parrish ranked at the top of Colby's suspect list. Visually he followed the middle-aged man's path as he meandered from one table to the next as if no worries existed in his life. Thin, tall, with gray hair, he puffed on a cigar, and despite the heat wore his trademark light-colored suit.

It took effort not to slug him. Since Parrish had arrived in town and announced that he was Harriet's estranged husband, he hadn't shown a second of genuine grief.

"Your mood is dark."

Colby turned slowly, preparing himself to see Tessa Madison's gray eyes. How could he have missed her? he thought. She wore a white dress with small pink and green flowers. Sleeveless, it brushed her ankles and scooped to a V above the shadow of her breasts, just enough to tempt his imagination. On her feet were white sandals with half a dozen straps. He eyed her pink toenails and the thin ring, a silver band, on one toe. "My mood's okay."

"Purple aura," she teased.

He found himself grinning. "Not green anymore?"

"Oh, no. Definitely purple."

Staring at her lips, not for the first time, he wondered about her taste. "Not a good sign?"

Slowly her smile spread to her eyes. "Certain auras reflect a person's mood or future."

Colby couldn't stop himself. He released a snort of disbelief.

"You don't believe that?"

He could do his own kind of taunting. "I believe in what I can see—" He paused, looked away from the gold triangle dangling from her left earlobe and fingered her necklace and the amulet, a dime-size letter X. "Touch." Deliberately he let his skin brush hers above the scooped neckline. "Feel." With satisfaction, he heard her suck in a breath as his knuckle caressed her skin. "What's this?"

"It's the runic letter for good luck." Her gaze remained on him as she stepped back, forcing the chain to slip from his fingers. "Are you here to buy something?"

"Browsing." Admiration whipped through him. She wouldn't intimidate easily. "What about you?"

"I bought something." When she gestured toward a cherrywood rolltop desk, a pleased smile lit her face. "Look. Isn't this beautiful?" Lovingly she ran a hand over the top of the desk.

"Nice." He had no real knowledge about what was a genuine antique, but he liked her choice. Not perfect, its top bore a few scratches. It had been more than a fine antique. It had been useful. Sturdy, long-lasting, it was also too heavy for her to move around. Colby viewed the moment as the perfect opportunity. "Do you need help getting it home?"

In a slow, measuring way, she cast a sidelong look at him.

He laughed, guessing her thought. "No strings."

"I couldn't ask you...."

"I volunteered."

"I have a van. I'll go home and get it."

"Do you have good muscles, too?" She looked like a good wind would knock her down. He watched her eyes slice to his arms, sinewy after years of pitting his strength against a broncing animal.

"Colby." Henry's slap on the shoulder forced him to look away. "I heard news." Henry spoke low, as if his news was confidential. "Diana's back."

Colby hadn't seen Diana in a year, not since the day she'd placed his engagement ring on the bedside table and announced she wanted something he wouldn't give her.

"I heard she's staying in town for a while, might even settle down here again."

"That so?"

Henry grinned wider. "Want me to tell her hi for you if I see her?"

"No, Henry." Colby chose a surefire way to get Henry to leave. "Give me a hand with this desk, will you?"

Henry looked so dumbfounded at the request that Colby nearly laughed.

"You don't have to," Tessa protested.

"It's yours?" Henry snuck a look to his left and then his right as if checking to see who was watching him. "Uh, sorry, Colby. Got to go. Lester needs me," he said about his brother.

Lester was nowhere in sight. "That's okay. I can manage by myself," Colby said.

"You shouldn't have asked him to help me," Tessa said once they were alone. "Most people aren't comfortable around me."

Because she made them believe she was weird. But was she? He stared at the desk. A sturdy, serviceable choice, the kind a practical person would favor. "This isn't about you. It's about his laziness."

"He mentioned your ex-fiancée, didn't he?"

"Diana Lynscot. She married another. Did you learn that, too?"

"Yes. I heard, too, that she's a widow now." Empathy filled her voice. "That's so terrible. To be a widow and not even be thirty."

"He was fifty-nine. And rich." He withdrew his truck keys from a pocket. "I'll get my truck and take this desk to your place, if you're ready to leave."

"I am. Thank you for playing good neighbor Sam." He watched long, soot-black lashes flutter before she raised her eyes to him. Enough. He needed to stop noticing every little thing about her. He had enough on his mind. Like his ranch. And a prize mare.

"The mare—" She started, then paused and looked past him.

The mare. His mare? What about her? He waited for her to say more, but she was smiling at someone.

Curious, Colby looked over his shoulder.

Slim, with chin-length dark hair, his mother strolled toward them with a bright smile. "Is he being difficult, Tessa?"

"No, he isn't, Louise," Tessa answered.

Colby slipped an arm around his mother's shoulder. "Quit talking about me as if I took a walk."

Her smile waned despite his humor. "Did you see *him?*"

"I saw him," he answered, well aware she was discussing Parrish. "Try to ignore him, Mom."

"I plan to." She craned her neck. "Your father is around here somewhere. He's thinking of buying one of those electric beer signs." She rolled her eyes. "I do hope I can talk him out of it." Lightly she touched Tessa's hand. "Nice to see you again, Tessa."

"You, too."

"I'll be by the store soon," she assured with a backhand wave.

Tessa looked in another direction. "That man." With a nod of her head, she indicated Parrish. "Is he the one who was casting gloom around you?"

"Casting gloom around me?" She had a cute way about her.

"That's what he was doing," she said, deadly serious.

"Yeah, that's Parrish." Temptation slithered through him to reach out, thread his fingers through silky-looking black hair. He wondered if the strands felt as soft as they looked. "Warren Parrish," he added and wondered if he was losing perspective, letting his attraction for her interfere with why he was with her. "Parrish came to town and claimed he was married to my aunt. Harriet had never mentioned him or being married."

"Have you checked this out?"

"They're doing that."

She met his gaze. "The sheriff?"

"Holt Tanner, the deputy sheriff, is checking on him." He didn't like having to sit back and let someone else handle everything. "So far there's no new leads, no real suspects. I'll get the truck." On the way home, he might stop at the vet's. The mare was prime for breeding but still wasn't pregnant.

"She is pregnant, you know."

It took a second for her words to sink in. This was nuts. He didn't believe she had some psychic vision about his horse. Over his shoulder, he leveled his best no-nonsense look at her. ''No, she isn't.'' He'd been informed a week ago that the test had been negative. He kept walking without another look back. She'd heard he was concerned about the mare. She was trying to mess with his head. Well, she was wasting her time. He didn't believe in psychics, karma, transcendental babble. He'd never even liked magic shows.

''Colby.'' Henry fell in step beside him. ''You need to know something.''

In no mood for conversation with Henry, he only slowed his stride instead of stopping. He wasn't twenty feet from his truck. The conversation would be brief, he hoped.

''People aren't too sure about her—that Tessa Madison.''

That stopped him. He'd never worried what other people thought about something that was his business. ''I didn't know you knew her well enough to have an opinion,'' Colby challenged. He'd always favored the underdog. That was his father's doing. Bud Holmes had studied law for a while before his father's death had forced him to take over the family ranch. He'd taught his son to believe in honesty and a fair chance for everyone. Colby figured Tessa Madison deserved one, too.

''Just telling you what I heard. She was arrested last year while living somewhere else. You might want to stay clear of her.''

Colby drilled a hard look at him. ''Sounds like gossip to me, Henry.'' What could she have done to be arrested? Fraud? A scam?

Henry started to move away. ''Don't say you weren't warned.''

Colby scowled after him, then unlocked his truck. Minutes later, with the help of the mayor, Pierce Dalton, he'd loaded the desk onto the bed of his truck.

''That was nice of the mayor,'' Tessa said while settling in the passenger's seat. ''People really like him.''

He picked up on her small talk. ''He's with Chelsea, you know,'' he reminded her.

She released a soft laugh, a soft and sensuous-sounding laugh. A laugh that sent a jolt through him. ''Yes, I do know that. They're planning a wedding. And no, I'm not interested in our mayor.''

Colby was surprised. A lot of single women in town were disappointed when Pierce got engaged to Chelsea. At the end of the block, Colby maneuvered the truck around the corner to her store.

''I have a furniture dolly at the store,'' she said as he braked.

Colby flicked off the ignition. Before he could respond, she jumped out of the truck. Was she always so high-energy or was he making her nervous? Meeting her on the sidewalk, he held out a hand. ''Give me the keys and—''

With an airy stride, she ambled ahead of him toward the back of the house. ''Don't need them.''

Okay, Rumor wasn't the crime capital of the nation, but good sense made most people lock doors. "Why don't you lock?"

"It doesn't work."

He said the logical thing. "Then buy a new one."

She stilled, grinned at him. "Why?"

"Don't you worry about a burglar?"

"Why should I? Only someone who believed in what I sell would be interested in my merchandise. At present, that number is few."

Logic. Amazing. She'd made her point with logic. "A woman alone should lock the door."

"I do plan to contact a locksmith," she assured him with a more serious look.

Colby liked her smile. "Did you have fun at my expense?"

"A little." She reached for the doorknob, opened the door but paused. "You've been warned about me, haven't you?"

He'd never put much faith in anything Henry said. "My mother thinks you're the best thing that's happened to this town."

A smile sprang to her face. "You're kidding?"

"A breath of fresh air."

"If only everyone thought that way," she said wistfully.

"Tessa, is that you?" The blonde with the sing-song voice charged into the storeroom. The moment she spotted him, she skidded to a stop. "Oh, hi."

Colby grinned. She looked surprised and flustered. "Hi." He'd had his share of rodeo groupies. It harmed no one for him to be pleasant.

Tessa lifted a brow but said nothing about her assistant's reaction. "I didn't think you'd still be here, Marla."

"Jolie and I were talking after I locked up. She wants to know if you think her ghost will like—"

Another voice interrupted. "Oh, don't bother her now." A carrot-colored redhead stood in the doorway that connected the storeroom to the front of the store. "Come on, Marla," Jolie said, and snagged the younger woman's arm to pull her into the store.

Colby waited until they were alone. "Her ghost?"

"She has a friendly one."

"Is there such a thing?"

"Some spirits are malevolent."

"How do you know if…" He stopped himself, not believing he was having a conversation about ghosts.

"I hope Marla and Jolie didn't make you uncomfortable. They aren't too subtle about their matchmaking. And they're always trying to find me my soul mate." A hint of humor sparkled in her eyes. "Regina, Marla's sister, assured me that love would only happen if it's in the stars."

In the stars. That kind of thinking belonged to a romantic. He wasn't one of them. "Isn't there some guy somewhere?"

"No, there isn't. Do you want to get the desk?"

"Sure." Before stepping away, he touched a corner of the old desk. "What about this one?"

"I'm moving it outside behind the store. The neighbor two doors down wants it."

Colby spent the next few moments transferring

desks. After moving the new one inside, he left to take the other one to her neighbor. The man rattled off a dozen thank-yous before Colby left. Returning to Tessa's store, he found her on the phone, frowning.

She set down the receiver, offered a weak smile. "Thank you for helping with the desks."

"It's okay." She had trouble, had no good reason to share it with him, but she looked as if she needed a sympathetic shoulder. "You have a problem?"

"You'll probably hear about it." She set a cup with a whimsical drawing of a black cat on the desk. "That was my landlady. Esther Dugan."

Esther had been his fourth-grade teacher. Never had he heard her say a harsh word to anyone. "I didn't know she owned the place." He wandered to a counter. "Sweet lady," he said, staring at a deck of tarot cards.

"I always thought so. She's also malleable." She strained for a smile. "It's not your problem."

He turned and perched on the edge of the desk. "I asked."

She shrugged. "She informed me that the rent is being raised and is due at the first of next month. I doubt I can pay that much of an increase. Perhaps six months from now when my business is more established and Mystic Treasures becomes known in Whitehorn and Billings."

"But not yet?"

"No. Eventually I'd hoped to buy the house." She plopped pens and pencils into the cup. "I'm sure that

Leone Burton influenced her. She's Esther's sister-in-law. Leone came in to see me and—''

''She came in here?'' He couldn't hide his incredulity. Set in her ways, even a touch narrow-minded, Leone came across as a lot older than fifty-something. She looked old-fashioned from her hairstyle, something that resembled a bun on the top of her head, to the laced-up shoes she always wore. In Colby's opinion, she'd be one of the last people in town to buy a crystal for seeing into the future.

''She's on a crusade to close my business.''

Colby didn't doubt Leone could manage to do that. Looking down, he stared at one of the tarot cards of two nudes. The Lovers was printed in bold black letters at the bottom of the card. Crazy. This was crazy. Too easily even he could fall beneath her whimsical spell. Annoyed, he dropped the lover's card. He wanted no part of love again. And he couldn't worry about her. He was here for his mother's sake. She was the one he needed to think about. ''What's this?'' He fingered a small vial of purple-colored liquid. ''A love potion?''

''Are you in need of one?''

Over his shoulder, he sent her a you've-got-to-be-kidding look. ''So what is this?''

''That's bath oil. It soothes. Relaxes sore muscles.''

He grinned with a thought. ''I've had more than my share of those.'' Facing her, he fished in his shirt pocket to withdraw photographs. It was time to force the issue. "Here. Look at the photos of my aunt, see what happens."

"Colby, I meant what I said earlier."

"That was then. Now you have a problem. And I have a solution. Two weeks," he said. He offered a generous amount of money for two weeks of her time, knew she needed it badly. "Think about it."

He didn't play fair. She could ignore his challenge but not the money. It would take care of the financial problem Esther had dropped in her lap. Still, during the two weeks he'd requested, her whole world could crumble around her. While she tried to identify Harriet's killer, she'd give Leone an opportunity to criticize her more, convince people she was a bad element for their town.

She placed a Closed sign in the store window, then returned to the table and spread out the photographs. The possibility existed that she might not see anything. She never could be certain she'd be able to help and she never knew how much pain she might feel.

Why hadn't she handed the photographs back to him? Why had she mentioned the mare, a pale beige horse with a white mane and tail? She'd made a mistake mentioning that horse. She'd had no reason to show off except to convince him she had power. Why was easy to answer. The attraction for Colby had descended on her so quickly, so intensely she'd had no chance to block it. It didn't matter that she hardly knew him or that they probably had nothing in common or that he belonged to a different world.

Most of all, he belonged.

And she was an outsider. She'd hoped if she didn't use her psychic ability she'd have a better chance at acceptance, would be able to stay in Rumor, make friends.

One of those friends was Louise Holmes, she reminded herself. How could she not help a friend? She placed fingers on one of the photos but felt nothing. She didn't think the photographs were recent enough to give her a clue about Harriet's killer.

If Winona Cobb and Crystal had been home, Tessa would have driven to Whitehorn to visit them, to see if they'd be more receptive. Like her, they'd weathered a storm of criticism because of psychic powers, but they and Crystal's husband, Deputy Sloan Ravencrest, were on vacation in California. So she'd try again. Stare harder. Let emotions radiate from the photos.

One of them was of Harriet decorating a Christmas tree. The ornament in her hand was a brass horn with a red and green plaid ribbon. Tessa closed her eyes. A foggy vision appeared of a young woman in a Victorian dress. An heirloom, Tessa guessed about the ornament. She felt peace. Joy. Love.

Another photograph was of Harriet and Louise smiling, sitting under a patio umbrella, frosty glasses of iced tea on the round table before them. A warm summer's breeze rustled leaves on the trees behind them. Tessa smelled lilacs, sensed affection and love between the sisters.

In the third photograph, Harriet and Henry, the

town's mayor years ago, stood before the library. It appeared to be a dedication of some sort. Harriet was distracted. Boredom? Tessa couldn't pinpoint the woman's feelings.

For forty minutes, she concentrated on the photographs, but nothing about them helped her name Harriet's killer.

The roll of her stomach reminded her that she hadn't eaten since breakfast. She gathered the photographs, set them on the kitchen table, then headed upstairs. She changed into a peach-colored, scooped-neck T-shirt, jeans and sneakers.

Half an hour ago, a drizzle had begun. Now rain plopped in a light but steady syncopated beat on the sidewalk outside her store.

After snatching her umbrella, she dashed to the van. Branches swayed beneath an angry wind. Storms rarely bothered her, but the day had carried more turmoil than usual. She was edgy. The moment she slid behind the steering wheel, she hit the button for her CD player.

As she drove, fingers of lightning reached downward, brightening the street with eerie flashes. Thunder rumbled, overpowering the lilting sounds of flutes and a Celtic melody.

She slowed the van, peered between the swishing windshield wipers, checked her rearview mirror for cars behind her. One followed at a distance. She passed the Calico Diner. Through one of the trailer's windows, she saw a server. Her dark hair shone beneath the lights. Tessa had planned on going in for a hamburger, but judging by the cars parked in the dirt lot outside the trailer with its fifties decor, the diner was crowded. She wasn't in the mood for that many people. She turned off the town's main street. She'd head home and search her refrigerator for dinner.

The headlights of the car behind her glared in her rearview mirror. She squinted. Was that the same car? Why would it be?

In a test of sorts, she sped up. The car closed in. Tightly she clutched the steering wheel. As she turned down another side street, the car followed. Why was someone following her? Though some people indicated displeasure about her store, no one had ever threatened her.

Yet earlier, while she'd looked at antiques, an uneasy sensation had crept up her spine. Despite the congenial greetings and the laughter generously sprinkled among conversations, people had seemed jumpy. She'd tried to ignore the feeling. At the time, she'd thought she was feeling their apprehension. But now she knew. There had been more. More than once, she had sensed ill will from someone in the crowd.

Was that person in the car behind her? She maneuvered around another corner and toward Main Street. People. She didn't want to drive all the way to the Calico Diner. But she needed people. Lots of people.

In the dark confines of the car behind her, desperation seized the driver. No chance could be taken. People were remembering how Winona Cobb's niece, Crystal, in Whitehorn, who was supposed to be psychic, had helped authorities after the Montgomery girl's death.

The possibility existed that Tessa Madison, too, had what people called sixth sense. Whatever was necessary had to be done to scare her off.

Her car stayed on Main Street, then turned into the parking lot adjacent to Joe's Bar. It looked packed with the expected Friday night crowd. Did she know she was being followed? That was good. If she was scared, she'd back off.

She'd better.

Chapter Three

Her heart pounding, Tessa rushed from her car with keys in one hand and her umbrella in the other. At the door of Joe's Bar, she glanced at the street. The car drove by. Had she imagined she was being followed? *No, don't doubt yourself.* She knew what she'd felt. She knew when to be afraid. And like it or not, she felt shaky. She needed to stay off the street until she'd calmed down.

Inside, the smell of stale tobacco and alcohol hung in the air. The dog greeted Tessa first. A black rottweiler named Joe who liked women. Tessa had gone to the bar with its rustic, dark wood decor only once before with Marla.

Wet from the run in the rain, Tessa dropped to her haunches to pet Joe. As she ran a hand over his silky black coat and patted his head, she scanned the noisy and crowded dimly lit room. She gave the dog a final pat, then weaved her way around tables toward an empty one near a dartboard and the pool table.

"Do you play?"

Instantly relief rushed through her. At the sound of Colby's voice behind her, she stopped mid-stride. Until that moment, she hadn't realized how much she'd needed someone familiar, a friendly face.

He flashed a smile at her. The rodeo champion smile, the smile that must have curled dozens of women's toes. At the bar, two men whispered. Tessa raised her chin a notch when the buzz of voices increased. Wherever she went in town that happened. She hoped with time that people would get used to seeing her and the whispers would stop.

In a fluid move, Colby passed the end of the bar and elbowed the stomach of a dark-haired cowboy who was perched on a bar stool. He wore the usual garb, a black Stetson, Western work shirt and jeans, but instead of boots, he had on black sneakers with purple stripes. In response to Colby's good-natured jab, his friend grunted instead of finishing what he'd started to say to his buddy.

"So do you play?" Colby asked again, bringing her attention to him.

Smiling over his friend's look of surprise, Tessa nodded. She liked the unpredictable and never turned down a reasonable dare. Striding by, she slid the pool stick from Colby's hand, then leaned over the green felt table. "Are we playing for something?"

Colby racked up the balls. "Beer and a pizza." To her delight, his voice trailed off as she made the break and sunk a ball into a corner pocket. Two more dropped into a side pocket.

Bent forward over the table, Tessa angled a smile over her shoulder at him. His gaze lingered on her backside in the tight jeans. "If I lose, I pay?" she asked.

He was slow to answer, slow to meet her stare. A woman knew when she was presenting her best side to someone. "No, if I win, I pay," he finally said.

Tessa couldn't help smiling even though she missed sinking the next ball. "And if I win?"

"I pay."

She laughed. "That's not too logical."

"Who said I have to be?"

You, she thought, but kept the seriousness at bay. She played to win, and lost only because she was distracted by a waitress and the smell of pizza on a tray. As the aroma of tomatoes and basil and sausage permeated the air, her stomach growled with hunger. "Is that our pizza?"

"You're drooling," he teased. "And yes, it's ours."

"You won, then." Tessa was already trailing the waitress to a corner table.

Behind her, she heard his chuckle. "I think you let me."

He had a nice laugh. A great smile. "How could I do that?" She decided she was definitely in trouble.

Lightly he placed a hand at the small of her

back to urge her toward the table. "You didn't distract me."

Tessa stifled a pleased grin. "How could I distract you?"

"You moved."

"That's your excuse?" With a tsk, she settled on a chair. "What kind of pizza?"

"Cheese and sausage."

"In Billings, there's a place that makes tofu pizza."

He straddled a chair beside hers. "Save me."

"I guess you don't like dim sum."

His brows angled. "I'm a cowboy."

She couldn't help laughing.

"Bet you like arty-far—those foreign movies with subtitles, too?"

"Romantic comedies. Sci-fi."

He made a face. If he'd been trying to find common ground, she thought he'd be wasting his time.

"You're not what I expected, you know. I thought you'd be—"

"Wearing a turban, chanting mumbo jumbo to the air?" she asked, cradling a slice of pizza with the tips of her fingers.

"You make it all sound stupid. But yeah, I guess that's what I expected. You tried to convince me that was true."

She'd thought he'd go away.

"Someone said you were born in Rumor. Where did you live after you left here?"

"We did a lot of traveling."

"A Gypsy fortune-teller's life?"

"How exotic sounding."

Picking up a slice of pizza, he shifted his body toward hers. "It wasn't like that?"

She smiled wide. "In some ways, it was a really normal life. For a while, my mother worked in a bank to earn a living for the two of us." She paused, glanced away as a cowboy in a black Stetson settled on a bar stool next to a fellow in a baseball cap. "She moved us away from Rumor when I was an infant."

"Now hometown girl returns. Why?"

"Why not? I never knew any place as home. You were right about one thing. We lived like vagabonds, always moving someplace new." Tessa saw no point in explaining how difficult her mother's life had been. Alone with an infant, viewed as strange, her mother had constantly searched for new beginnings. Every move had been about starting over. After her death, Tessa had vowed no more. She'd chosen Rumor because her mother had once been a part of this town. She planned to stay, and nothing Leone Burton or anyone else did would weaken her resolve.

"Why did you move so much?" He stretched long legs beneath the table.

He appeared relaxed, but she felt tense—because of him. A quicker heartbeat, a slight flutter in her stomach, a twinge of need signaled just how much he affected her. "Because my mother would have a vision. Then people wouldn't want us around. The ability to see is something all the women on my mother's side share. It's hereditary." She spoke with pride. She wasn't ashamed of her ability, but it made relationships difficult. Like her mother, she'd had trouble whenever she'd gotten too close to someone. It was better to keep a distance. That was a lesson she'd learned early. "I heard you retired from rodeo recently."

"Too many injuries. Like the dislocated shoulder."

There was more. He harbored something heavy, Tessa realized. Something far more painful than a rodeo injury. If she concentrated, she could have learned his secret, but she would never intrude on another's pain without being asked. "How did it happen?"

"After tossing me, the bull decided to give me a nudge."

He made it sound as everyday as crossing the street. "You've lived a dangerous life."

"It can be."

"So you quit to stay safe?"

"That makes sense, doesn't it?" Disturbingly his gaze swept over her face, settled on her mouth.

"Yes," Tessa said. She resisted an urge to wet her lips.

"Have you thought about my offer?"

"You made it impossible to resist." The door opened, and Tessa looked to see who was coming in. Would she sense the person who'd been in the car behind her? "I looked at the photographs. Does your mother have a flower garden?" With his nod, she went on. "Are there lilacs?"

"Lilacs?" His voice carried a trace of bafflement. "What do they look like?"

As a young boy, had he picked some for his mother? "A cluster of small, purple flowers."

"There used to be. What kind of flowers do you like?"

Tessa ignored his question. "I had a sense of lilacs when I looked at one photo." She'd thought that particular photo had been taken in Louise's backyard.

"That's twice you've done that."

"Done what?"

"We were talking about you, not me and not the photos. You deliberately dodge."

"The photos are why we're together."

Unexpectedly he leaned forward, touched a strand of hair near her cheek.

The casual touch was as good as a caress. He could make her feel all she'd avoided for years. She knew that as sensation slithered over her.

"What else did you learn from them?"

She'd show caution, wouldn't make too much of his every touch. "I want you to know that I can never be certain I'll be successful. But I'll need your help. If it's not too difficult for you, I need you to tell me about the murder."

As if taking a moment to formulate his words, he sipped his beer. "I don't know how much you read about it in the newspaper. Chelsea estimated that Harriet was killed on June thirtieth, the night of the lunar eclipse. Harriet was shot with a twenty-two, her own.

Chelsea thinks she was knocked around first." His voice suddenly sounded tight.

"You don't have to tell me more if you don't want to."

For a second, he looked away, then went on as if she'd said nothing. Tessa assumed he was sidestepping emotion. "My aunt was hit on the back of the head. She was found in a chair, so he must have moved her there. Her lip was split. There must have been quite a fight before he shot her."

"Are you sure it's a man?"

"That's an assumption."

"You said that—" Tessa paused as Warren Parrish strolled in. Had he been the one following her?

Colby swung a look over his shoulder to trace her stare. "Son of a—"

Wearing a suit, Warren Parrish looked out of place among the casually dressed, mostly jeans-clad crowd.

Across the room, his stare met Colby's. Tessa wondered if the man had a death wish as he crossed the room to stop beside their table.

Though Colby kept his eyes on her, they grew darker with anger. "What do you want?"

Parrish looked pasty, almost sickly to Tessa. "I want to know when the lawyer will be reading Harriet's will."

In a slow, deliberate way, Colby raised his head. "After you're in jail."

"If you keep trespassing on what will be my property, you might be the one who ends up in jail."

Under his breath, Colby muttered a vile curse. For

an instant, Tessa thought he would whirl Warren toward him and punch him. Instead he followed Parrish with his eyes as if willing him to get out of his sight. "Did you get any—whatever it is you get—vibrations when he was around?"

Tessa wished she had. "No vibrations. Don't you think it odd that Harriet never told her sister when she got married?"

Some of the anger lingered in his voice. "Right now, we only have his word about his marriage to Harriet. It's possible they weren't. Holt's checking on that," he said, sounding less irritated.

"You told me Chelsea had a personality profile. What is it?"

"The killer is mature. She thought he might be military or in an elected position, a CEO or a cop. Someone with authority."

"Does that profile fit Warren Parrish?"

"He was a sergeant in the Army at one time."

Tessa watched him sprinkle Parmesan on a slice of pizza. "Who else is on the suspect list?"

"An unknown lover. And an abusive husband of a woman my aunt helped. At least, my mother thinks he's a possibility. Like Parrish, the guy was in the Army. An MP. So he fits the profile."

She considered all he'd said. "Did the sheriff's department come up with a motive for the killing?"

"By Rumor standards, my aunt was fairly rich. I guess Warren's motive would be an inheritance. He arrived in town to wait for the reading of the will. The lover? Who knows? The talk at the sheriff's office is that Aunt Harriet was blackmailing him, demanding money for her silence about the baby. That doesn't make sense to me. She had money. The other possibility was that she was demanding marriage, and he wanted no part of her or the baby.''

"And the abusive husband? His motive is obvious,'' she said absently. "Revenge because Harriet interfered in what he'd consider was his business.''

"Right.'' He wiped his hands on a napkin. "Tell me. When did this—the images—start?''

She'd expected the question. Everyone, even those who didn't believe in her, asked. "When I was a child.'' She needed no images to remember childhood taunts. Some people had called her crazy.

"Just like that, one day you woke up and saw things?''

She wasn't offended by the skepticism in his voice. Only someone with ESP understood. Some people felt only a vague foreboding, which they excused as intuition. But even they comprehended how overpowering the moment was when what was real was suspended by a world in the future. "It came in funny ways,'' Tessa said. "I'd be playing with a friend, and I'd tell her the telephone was going to ring. She thought it was wonderful I could do that, but her mother looked at me as if I'd grown an extra head.'' She paused with another memory. "When we were living in Texas, another friend's mother called to tell my mother that I was a witch and she didn't want me near her daughter. Different scares people.''

"Why did she think you were a witch? What did you do?"

He would believe what he wanted. Long ago she'd learned she couldn't always convince people about her gift. "I was eleven when I told her daughter, a schoolmate, that her dad was going to have a flat tire. No one paid attention until after he hit the streetlight because of a blowout. Fortunately no one was hurt, but the family was convinced I caused it, cast a spell."

"Jerks."

Had he said that because he didn't believe in spells, or because they'd been so judgmental?

"Chelsea said she met you in Chicago. Something about how you helped the police with a case."

Since Chelsea had revealed that much, Tessa had little choice except to tell him what had happened. "Several women had been killed in the same way. Everyone believed there was a serial killer. An employee at the mall where I was working was one of them. Because I was acquainted with her, I began to have dreams—nightmares."

"So the visions are dreams?"

"Sometimes. It can happen in the middle of the day, too. But this time, the visions came at night. The last one I saw…" She stopped, made herself go on. "She was happy, laughing with friends. Tall, blond, lovely. She'd been dancing. I felt her fear and pain when he grabbed her, wrapped an arm around her neck." She stopped, drew a hard breath. The feelings were almost on her again with the remembrance. "He was choking her. She was terrified."

"You saw her killed?"

She met his stare. "No, I never saw her killed. That's why I went to the police. I knew then that I was seeing something that would happen."

"Could you describe her? Where she was?"

"No. Him. I saw him. Chelsea was the forensic expert on the case. She believed in me more than the detectives. She talked to an old-timer. He had me sit with a police artist, describe him. The police picked up a man who'd had a police record. I told Chelsea the fibers she found at two of the crime scenes were from a navy peacoat he owned. They'd find it stuffed in a steamer trunk in an uncle's garage. They got a warrant, but there was no steamer trunk."

His brows bent in a frown.

"You're wondering why I'm telling you this. I'm not always successful."

"Did they ever convict him?"

"Yes, they did. They couldn't hold him, but after a few weeks, he tried again. This time someone was around before he hurt anyone." Tessa didn't bother to tell him the woman was tall, blond, looked exactly like the one in her nightmare. He wouldn't believe that really happened. He didn't want to. And she didn't tell him that they'd found the coat, just as she'd said in a steamer trunk, or that it was in the garage of a stepuncle in another state.

"Why did you come here?"

Tessa looked at him over the rim of a beer glass. "You mean in Joe's Bar? Or to Rumor?"

"Both." She glanced at the door again. Could she have imagined someone following her? Laughing, a twenty-something couple wearing matching leather pants and spiked hairdos strolled in. "I came to Rumor because I want a home, I want to settle down." She yearned for a place to belong, and she wondered if decades from now she'd still be longing for that.

"What about here?" He held out a hand, palm up. "Why did you come in here?" He gave her that slow, easy grin that had undoubtedly kick started a fair share of female hearts.

Tessa rolled her eyes. "Oh, I don't believe it. You think I came in here because I saw your truck?"

"Did you?"

"Your ego is showing," she answered, but if she'd noticed the truck, she knew she might have stopped at Joe's to see him again.

"You're bruising it."

She turned away to hide a smile. She didn't want him to be too charming, too attractive.

He took a hearty swallow of his beer. At a nearby table, a couple in cowboy hats called to him, mentioned a rodeo. The woman gave Colby a little flirtatious wave. While he shared a laugh with them, Tessa glanced toward the entrance for the umpteenth time.

"Hey." Colby waved a hand up and down in front of her. "Who are you looking for? You keep checking the door."

She mustered a smile. "Was I?"

"Level with me. You look uneasy every time someone comes in. Why?"

Tessa wanted to tell someone about the car. "I was followed here."

"Followed?" His brows bunched. "Someone was really following you?" Obviously he didn't expect her to answer the question. "Who?"

Head bent, she made much of wiping a napkin across greasy fingers. "I don't know. I should have tried to see who it was, but I wasn't thinking about that. I wanted to be with other people. Being followed is always a worry for a woman driving alone at night."

"This was more. You know that, and so do I. When we were at the antiques sale, people were assuming because you were with me that you were helping me. I never gave a thought to the idea that someone might feel threatened." He paused, nodded a hello to two men passing by to the bar. "Do you want to back out?"

After trying to persuade her to work with him, just like that, he asked if she wanted to stop. He had a nice soft center. She'd never say that to him, though. "I don't scare so easily."

"Glad to hear that, but…"

His voice faded. Images came with no warning. Two men. Embracing? Wrestling? A Stetson sailed through the air. She heard a barking dog. A rottweiler. Here. The images were here. "We should leave," Tessa urged.

Colby rounded a look over his shoulder and traced her stare to the bar. "Is one of the guys there the one who followed you?"

"No." Tessa stood and reached for her umbrella.

"But one of them bothers you? Bad aura?"

She knew he thought she was out of sync with the rest of the world. "The guy in the Stetson is going to sit on your lap."

He released a deep chuckle. "No way."

Tessa didn't bother to argue. Soon enough he'd learn she was right. "We'd better leave. Or..." She didn't bother to say more. It was too late.

At the bar, the guy in the baseball cap swung his arm and smashed his fist into the cowboy's chin. As the cowboy's head jerked back, the Stetson flew off. He spun and sailed in Colby's direction.

"Damn," Colby muttered. His hands went up, blocked the cowboy from landing across his lap. With a hard push, he propelled the cowboy toward the guy in the baseball cap. "Let's get out of here." Rising, he snagged her hand and propelled her toward the exit, toward the rottweiler, barking.

She laughed as he led the way. "Told you."

"How did you know they were going to fight? Lucky guess, right? Body language stuff," he mumbled as if talking to himself. "You read something in the way those fools were standing, looking at each other."

He was trying so hard to explain what happened. She realized then that nothing he was told would make him believe. He'd need irrefutable proof about her. "Could be." She preceded him outside and raised her face to the rain, though she held her umbrella. The air felt cool but smelled musty. In the distance, fingers of lightning stabbed toward the ground. A fire alert was on. The woods were dry.

"Where are you parked?"

She pointed to her right. "Over there." Before she could protest, he caught her hand in his. Tessa felt the strength, the calluses in the hand wrapped around hers.

"Why are you carrying the umbrella?"

"It's only drizzling."

He grinned in the manner of someone who didn't understand but was amused by another person's action. He probably thought she wasn't very sensible. She could have told him she took a daily vitamin, always carried an umbrella on cloudy days, wrote on a calendar the due dates of bills so she wouldn't forget to pay them in time. She was sensible, practical, normal—except she saw visions.

"I'll follow."

Tessa balked, stopping him. "Follow?"

"Don't even think about arguing."

"What would be the point?" Why would she argue when she was so grateful for the escort home?

He did more than follow her home.

"It's nice of you to walk me to the door," Tessa said when she paused with him on the short landing at the second floor.

Colby reached around her to open the door. "I'm coming in."

The thank-you riding Tessa's tongue remained unsaid. He stepped in ahead of her and began working his way through each room. "Find anyone?" she called.

Grinning, he entered the kitchen. "Not even a ghost. You need locks." He sniffed the air. "What is that smell?"

"I make poultices and sell them in the store." His look of disbelief didn't go unnoticed. "There are a lot of healthy ways to cure things besides drugs," Tessa added.

He said nothing, but she assumed that someone who followed traditional paths would have trouble with what she'd said. Her hair dripping, Tessa tugged at a wet strand and wandered into the bathroom for a towel. "Where was the Christmas photo taken?" she called.

"In Boston. Why?"

Briskly she rubbed the towel over her wet hair. "Harriet was in love then, wasn't she?"

"I guess."

Because his voice sounded near, she yanked the towel off her head. His hair glistening with dampness, he stood in the doorway, blocking it. "You're all wet." She tossed him the towel, and as he went to grab it, she stepped around him quickly to the kitchen. Pausing beside the table, she touched one of the photos, determined to keep a strictly business relationship between them. "These weren't recent enough for me to learn anything."

"But you saw something?"

"Images." She took a quick breath at his nearness. Standing beside her, he dragged the towel over his wet hair. "What images?"

"Sometimes smells come with them. Pine came through clearly when I touched the Christmas photo," she said, looking at it. "I have precognition, knowing of something in advance, of its happening, is the way it's scientifically explained, and—"

"You see something that's going to happen. Are they foggy images?"

"Foggy images?" She met dark brown eyes. "Dreams, I thought, when younger. Actually they seemed like nightmares then, because I didn't understand what was happening. And I can see by touching objects."

"And people?"

"Yes." Was she imagining how close his lips were to hers? So close. All she had to do was stretch, press her mouth to his. "Sometimes." Too much about him made her want to relax, be herself. That wouldn't be smart. She didn't want more hurt. She really didn't want this. She needed to keep her mind on her store. She wanted no emotional involvement with any man. "Colby, you should leave."

With a featherlight touch, he brushed strands of hair from her cheek in the manner of someone needing to touch. "I'll leave." He leaned toward her. Before she realized what he planned to do, he lowered his head and kissed her. It was a quick kiss, a mere brush of his lips across hers, but Tessa felt heat radiate down to her toes, sensed the passion he effortlessly could raise within her.

"My leaving won't end this. You know that."

Colby braked on the gravel driveway outside his ranch house and climbed out of his truck. Something was happening he hadn't expected and couldn't explain. She wasn't the scatterbrain he'd envisioned. And it didn't matter that they probably had nothing in common. He wanted her. It had been a long time since he'd wanted a woman's sweetness. There had been women to satisfy a physical need, but since he'd walked into her store, he hadn't stopped thinking about her. Maybe she'd hexed him.

She claimed to be a psychic, not a witch, he reminded himself. But what was the difference? How did he know? Hadn't one of her customers mentioned a ghost? What kind of world did she belong to? To him, ghosts belonged with goblins and other scary creatures on Halloween. Logical people didn't talk about them on a hot summer day in July.

How much should he believe of what she'd said regarding her mother, the women in her family having psychic powers? She could be feeding him nonsense about a childhood filled with visions of things about to happen to make him believe in her.

No, he didn't believe that. In all honesty, he thought she believed her claims about her special power. Some people were intuitively smart. She might be one of them. That made sense.

Slowly he wandered into his kitchen, aware of the ticking of the clock. He'd never minded being alone. He was comfortable with his own company. When traveling the rodeo circuit, he used to search for places to be alone.

With a beer in his hand, he ambled to the back porch. The silence bothered him tonight. He settled on the swing to concentrate on the plopping sound of the rain instead of his own thoughts. But his imagination played tricks on him. He heard a laugh, a soft, feminine laugh—Tessa's laugh. It rippled on the night air as if taunting him.

Maybe she had cast a spell.

Chapter Four

Unable to sleep past dawn the next morning, Colby grabbed a cup of coffee, then spent the first few hours after sunrise cleaning out stalls. He worked up a sweat, thought about the cost of a new roof for the barn, considered a drive to Whitehorn to see a movie that evening, looked for anything to distract him. But when he finished his chores hours later, he was still thinking about Tessa, about a kiss that had only tempted and made him want more.

After a cold shower, he gave up and drove toward town. This was downright crazy. He didn't believe in what she was, what she believed. He kept telling himself to go home, but then he was driving down Main Street and parking in front of Mystic Treasures. Muttering under his breath, he climbed out of his truck. Nothing made sense these days, including his actions.

He looked for an excuse for being there and crossed the street to the massive two-story brick building that housed Rumor's police department. Holt Tanner, the deputy sheriff, sat behind one of the steel, beige-colored desks. Tall with black hair, he had a brooding quality that Colby guessed the ladies found exciting. An ex-city cop, Holt intimidated a few folks in town. Colby liked the man's straightforward way. With a few short sentences, Holt filled Colby in on the latest news of his investigation into Harriet's death. "Figured you'd want to know right away. I received verification of a marriage between your aunt and Warren Parrish."

That wasn't news he wanted to hear. "Harriet really was married to him?"

Holt gave a slow nod and stood to wander toward the exit with him. "When they were both living in Boston. I have the name of a neighbor," he said as they stepped outside. "I might be able to learn more from her, but I haven't had a chance to call her yet."

"Let me," Colby urged. He looked past Holt. Across the street, Tessa whisked out of the shoemaker's. She had the best walk he'd ever seen. He gave his head a small shake. When had he ever been so enchanted with the way a woman looked when walking? He regarded her legs in the washed-out jeans, eyed the skimpy leather straps of her sandals. Several gold chains hung at the V of her black sleeveless top, and a bright purple sash draped her waist. "Give me the phone number. A neighbor might be willing to tell more to one of Harriet's relatives than to a cop.''

''We'll both give this a try.'' Holt handed Colby a sheet of paper with the phone number. ''Make sure you get back to me with whatever she says.''

Colby scowled at the number. How would he tell his mother that Harriet had actually married that slime? Damn, why had she? Was she that desperate for a man? At forty-three, Harriet had come across as strong, independent. Yet she'd chosen Parrish. But why was she in Rumor without him?

Colby had been raised by people who believed in their marriage vows. Thirty-six years after their wedding, his parents still acted in love. His father brought his mother flowers, grabbed her hand when crossing a street, snatched a kiss before he left the house. Never would they consider a long-distance relationship.

Steps from Mystic Treasures, Colby slowed his stride. Sunlight glaring in his eyes, he squinted at the long white box propped against the door. A florist's box.

He climbed the stairs to the porch, then bent and reached for the box. The card was addressed to Tessa Madison. As he stared at the box, a tinge of something twisted his stomach. He had no problem naming the emotion. He was jealous, and that made no sense at all.

He'd never even dated her. They'd shared one kiss. Hell, it wasn't even a kiss, not really. But he knew what he was feeling. He knew he wanted to crush the lid on the box and ram it in the closest garbage can.

Don't drool, Tessa, she warned herself when she spotted Colby waiting on the porch for her. He looked luscious in snug-fitting jeans and a chambray shirt. With a slower stride, she climbed the stairs.

Perhaps this attraction for him was nothing more than a need for affection. She truly missed the physical contact with a man. Not sex, but touch—the warmth of his hand around hers, the heat of his palm against the small of her back, the caress of a kiss against her lips.

"Hi," he said when she reached the top step.

She nodded but sensed something was wrong. He was upset. About what? While leaving the shoe-maker's shop, she'd seen him come out of the sheriff's office with Holt. "Has the sheriff's office learned more?"

"Guess these were just delivered," he said, holding out the box and acting more interested in talking about the flowers.

"For me?" Frowning, Tessa accepted the box. Who would send her flowers? She squeezed around him to open the door. She hadn't dated since returning to Rumor.

Stepping inside, she spotted the envelope tucked beneath a red ribbon on the box, but shook off a curious impatience to read the card. "What did Holt say that upset you?"

He stilled steps behind her. "How did you—you saw us talking, didn't you?"

Always he looked for an explanation. "Yes, I did," she called as she headed to the storeroom.

"And you assumed it wasn't good news," he said, trailing her.

Tessa merely smiled. He really resisted the concept of clairvoyance. "What did he tell you?"

"That Parrish was telling the truth. He and Harriet were married."

Tessa set the box on what used to be the kitchen counter. "It seems strange that they weren't living together." Her head bent, she stood with her back to him and slid the card from its envelope.

"Not the actions of two people who can't live without each other."

Tessa knew he'd said something, but his words didn't register. She couldn't look away from the card in her hand.

"Secret admirer?"

With his gentle touch on her shoulder, she swung a look at him and held up the card. Beneath her fingers, she felt anger. Such anger from the sender. "It's blank." Danger for her was near, she knew. "What will you do now that you know they were married?" she asked to try to distract herself.

"There's a neighbor in Boston. Maybe she'll know more."

Her heart went out to him. He hid his pain well, but his sorrow teetered close to the surface. "That would be good." She had to stop being so receptive to him. Years ago she'd allowed her guard to drop with a man. She'd left herself vulnerable to hurt. Her ex-boyfriend, Seth, had taught her a lesson that she didn't dare forget.

Giving in to curiosity, she lifted the lid on the box. Someone wanted to send a message. Brown, dried-out flowers were nestled in the green tissue.

Uneasy, she dropped the card on the counter. Was all this happening because she'd become involved in Harriet's killing, or was someone trying to discourage her from staying in business?

"Someone's idea of funny?" Colby said, peering over her shoulder.

"Not very."

"No, not very." Inclining his head, he forced her eyes to meet his. "Who told you that you always had to be brave?"

She gave him a weak smile. "Is that what I'm doing?"

"That's what it looks like to me."

"I'm all right," she insisted, but she wasn't. Someone was trying to frighten her, and was succeeding.

The heat of his breath flowed across her face. "If you need someone to lean on—" Lightly he pressed his hand against the small of her back. "I'm strong." He smiled, a full one that bracketed the corners of his mouth with deep grooves. "Reliable."

And too sexy, Tessa mused. She waited a moment to make sure her voice was steady. "Colby, I'm not easy to be with."

"High maintenance?"

When necessary, she chose the protectiveness of her crackpot image. "Our auras clash."

"Do they?" A tease sprang into his eyes, warmed them.

"It's a warning." She thought he should wear a warning. *Stay clear of this man. He breaks hearts.*

"Fine." His hand touched her arm, gently tugged it to bring her close. "I've been warned."

Her heart beating harder, she placed a palm against his chest. She wanted to laugh, make light of the moment, but she couldn't talk. Even as she took deep, calming breaths, she still wanted him to kiss her, really kiss her. "You're much too sensible, and I'm much too—"

A fingertip pressed to her lips, silencing her. "Fascinating."

Oh, don't be too charming, she wanted to plead. She watched his eyes flick to her mouth. Was he going to kiss her? Would one kiss end her desire for it? *Don't want it,* she railed at herself, but as he lowered his head and his mouth hovered near hers, she nearly moaned in anticipation.

Against her cheek, she felt his smile, then slowly his lips tasted one corner of hers. As he tangled his fingers in her hair, he nibbled at her bottom lip. She needed to think. This wouldn't work. She struggled to remember that. It would only complicate everything. If she stopped now, there would be no chance for that. "Colby—"

A slow smile tugged up the edges of his lips. "Since I left, I've been thinking about kissing you."

Tessa drew a deep breath. She didn't want to think about the threats or Leone. She didn't want to think about what Seth had done. Mostly she wanted to stop fantasizing about how great Colby's kiss would be.

When his lips pressed down on hers, she coiled her arms around his neck. As long as she kept thinking about him doing this, she'd never be able to keep everything only business between them. They'd kiss and feel nothing.

Instantly she knew she was wrong. His firm, hard mouth slanted across hers in a long, lingering kiss as if savoring. He made her pulse pound harder, her body hum. He made her ache. Worse, he made her think of an old dream, one filled with love.

When he pushed his tongue past her teeth and into the warmth of her mouth, her legs went weak. She was feeling too much. Too much excitement. Too much temptation. An urge to deepen the pressure, to sample more of his taste swarmed in on her.

A soft moan escaped from her throat. She'd imagined nothing. She recognized the danger ahead for her but didn't pull away. She absorbed every sensation, and as she relished his taste, she hungered with a greediness she hadn't known before.

With one kiss, he rippled an excitement through her that she'd vowed to stay clear of ever since Seth had been a part of her life. But Colby wasn't like Seth. At the moment, whether or not Colby believed in her didn't matter. With a clarity that seized her breath, she knew that if she let them, they would get closer. The hurt would come.

And he *would* break her heart.

Amazingly, with a kiss, he made bells ring in her head. Silly thought. No, it wasn't, she mused, working her way back from a sweet lethargy and an urge never to think again, only feel.

Again she heard bells. One bell, she realized. The bell above the entrance door. With a jerk, she shot a look at the door. And saw Leone Burton.

Definitely she didn't need this. Didn't she have enough trouble with this woman? She'd need her wits around Leone. A member of the town council, influential, Leone Burton was a mighty opponent. "You need to leave," Tessa whispered, a bit breathless as weakness still flooded her body.

Colby glanced from her to Leone Burton and back. "I'll stay."

"No." Tessa fired a warning look at him. He needed to leave. She couldn't deal with him and Leone Burton at the same time. "I want you to leave—now."

"Hell." She heard him mutter before he swung around. "Mrs. Burton." Colby nodded, slowed for a second. "Sure is hot. Everyone is looking forward to it cooling off."

Leone sent a chiding look at Tessa. "That's all her doing. You caused all this heat," she said to Tessa, unaware Colby had stalled behind her in the doorway for a second. As he went out the door, he looked amused. He thought Leone was fooling. Tessa knew better.

Leone had geared up to blame her for anything and everything. Tessa doubted the woman's hostility toward her was personal, since they hardly knew each other. Possibly Leone viewed anything New Age as too strange. "Is there something you want, Mrs. Burton?"

Dressed in a heavily starched white blouse buttoned to the neck and a gray skirt, she didn't look fazed by the heat. Her gray hair was sleekly bound in a chignon. She possessed light blue eyes, cold eyes. "I understand you've applied to have a booth for this store at Rumor's Cooling Off celebration."

Well, here goes. "I hope to become more a part of this community."

"I thought I made myself clear before this." Her icy stare never strayed from Tessa. "I plan to do everything in my power to prevent that. We don't need such nonsense like this on display," she said with a wide sweep of her arm toward the display of colored crystals. "I will call Sheriff Reingard if you force me to."

Tessa lifted her chin a notch. She didn't scare off easily. "I'm—" She paused, distracted by a noise at the back door. Frowning, she looked back. She wasn't expecting any deliveries.

"Don't you turn away from me," Leone reprimanded.

Tessa faced her. She needed to finish this conversation.

"I'm not through talking to you. Stay away from Colby Holmes. Don't try your spells on him."

"My spells?" Did this woman truly believe she possessed such power?

"His family is well thought of in this community. You aren't their kind." Leone pivoted, not waiting for a response and apparently not interested in one. Head high, she marched toward the door.

You aren't their kind. Funny. No matter how often she heard those words, they always hurt.

Annoyance stayed with Colby. Each time he was with her, he felt desire growing stronger. Each time he left her, he wanted to turn around and go back to her. No amount of reasoning explained what he felt. There were plenty of women who'd be thrilled if he paid attention to them. She sure as hell couldn't pretend she'd felt nothing. Her breathing hadn't been any steadier than his. He could barely think while kissing her. Even now, all he could remember was the taste of her.

One day he'd kiss her, and she wouldn't push him away, act as if it meant nothing. It wasn't a damn crime to have someone see him kissing her, but she'd acted as if they'd be shot. Just because Leone—

Colby stilled in mid-stride. Damn, but he was dumb. This wasn't about him. Hadn't she told him that Leone was determined to make trouble for her? Muttering an explicit oath, he did an about-face.

"Colby."

He looked up. Feet away, coming out of Sylvia's dress shop, his mother sent him a wide smile. "Are you on your way to Mystic Treasures?" She had that matchmaking gleam in her eye that always put him on alert.

"That's where I'm headed."

"Wonderful." She drew a tissue from the pocket of her beige tailored pants and dabbed at the perspiration above her upper lip.

More determined to get some answers than give them, he slowed his stride to walk with her. "Did you know Tessa's mother?"

"We weren't good friends, but I talked to her. Cassandra was a little wild. I was dull in comparison." She released a short laugh. "Can you imagine?"

He smiled with her. "Not really." People gravitated toward his mother because of her bright smile and friendliness.

She turned a speculative look at him. "Why are you asking about her?"

"I wondered what kind of mother she was to Tessa." In comparison to Tessa's childhood, he'd guess that his life had been more stable. His parents were steady. Reliable. Loving.

A smile remained on his mother's face. "I'd only known her briefly."

"You liked her," he guessed.

"Very much."

He liked that about his mother, her ability to see the best in people.

"She was pregnant then, and you were four. So we talked about our children, as most young mothers would, and then I left to be with your father. He was in the Marines at that time. I was more interested in a home and being a wife and mother than she was. Though pregnant, she conveyed that she planned to travel. I thought she wasn't very responsible."

"Do you think Tessa is like her mother?"

"Of course not. Tessa isn't flighty like her. She's a very responsible young woman. She's a lot like Harriet."

Now there was a comparison he would never have considered.

"Harriet helped people like the Mason sisters. Only a few people knew about what she'd done. Tessa, too, is like that. She volunteers at Whitehorn Memorial. And weeks ago, she took in a widow with her two children who needed a place to stay until insurance money came through."

Why hadn't people heard about that?

"Were you at the sheriff's office?"

"And Tessa's."

"Really?" A speculative gleam entered her eyes. "If you were at Tessa's already, why are you going back?"

Colby figured she didn't need to know everything. "Someone came in to see her."

"Oh, Colby," she said in a tone so reminiscent of one she'd used when he was a kid that he almost felt guilty without knowing why. "Some other man is already seeing her?"

Since his relationship with Tessa was based on a couple of kisses, he thought it best to remind her. "I'm not seeing her that way, Mom."

She gave him her best reprimanding look. "I told

you about her, told you to get to know her. So who was visiting her?''

"Leone Burton.''

Her reprimanding look turned into one of good-natured annoyance. "You made me believe it was a man.''

"You made that assumption,'' he teased as she climbed the steps of Mystic Treasures with him.

"Sometimes you're too much like your father,'' she said, laughter edging her voice. But her smile slipped quickly. "Leone, you said. That's not good news for Tessa.''

"I heard she wants the store closed.''

"What she really wants is Tessa tarred and feathered and run out of town.''

He reached around her to open the door to the store. "Seriously.''

"Seriously,'' his mother said before preceding him inside.

Colby noticed Leone was gone. The soft strains of Celtic music filled the store. Head bent, Tessa stood in the storeroom at the coffee brewer. In response to the ding of the bell above the door, she looked at them.

His mother swept toward her. "Tessa, hello.''

While they met like old friends, exchanging a hug, Colby stayed in the main part of the store.

His mother beamed when Tessa complimented her about her bright orange short-sleeve blouse. "Clothes are why I'm here. There's an adorable dress that came into Sylvia's in your size," his mother said about Sylvia's Boutique where she was working part-time.

Colby waited near a display. Love potions. Did people really buy them? He looked up as his mother wandered out of the storeroom with Tessa.

"Did I tell you that Tessa predicted Sylvia would get married?"

"I thought you didn't predict," Colby reminded her.

At his challenge, a frown shadowed her eyes. "No one needed a crystal ball to tell they were in love. And Louise played matchmaker."

He didn't doubt his mother had guided her best friend in the direction of Larry, a Marine buddy of his father's who'd moved to Rumor to work with Colby's dad on the ranch.

"Yes, that's true. But Tessa knew," her mother said firmly. Clearly she really believed in Tessa's power. For a few moments, she shared with Tessa a humorous story about Sylvia and Larry's first meeting. "I'll be leaving now," she announced. "So you two can be alone."

Colby watched her breeze out the door. "My mother has grandmotherly visions," he said, moving close.

"You don't have to explain." She smiled with him. "I didn't expect you back."

"I came back because of unfinished business," he said quietly.

"Unfinished—" Her eyes met his briefly.

As she started to look away, he crowded her. He

wanted her taste again. Teasing both of them, he brushed his lips over hers. He was a second away from deepening the kiss when the bell above the door rang again. Annoyance skittered through him. Under his breath, he muttered a curse at another interruption. What would it take to get time alone with her?

Beaming, Tessa's assistant strolled in holding hands with a guy Colby had seen around town. A traveling salesman for a tool company, he dealt mostly with the town's hardware store. Tall, fair-haired, all teeth when he smiled, he probably appealed to women who liked dimples. Colby checked Tessa's reaction. She wasn't one of them, he guessed. She shook the guy's hand and nodded at Marla's request. She seemed to be forcing a smile.

"So I'll be back in a few hours," Marla rattled on. "Thanks a lot, Tessa, for letting me have time off."

"Go." She offered another strained smile.

"She's special to you?" Colby asked the moment they were alone.

"Like a sister."

"What bothers you about the guy that was with your friend?"

She tucked a strand of hair behind her ear. "How do you…?"

"You wear your emotions."

Frustration edged her voice. "He could hurt her."

"That's a chance everyone takes when they meet someone new."

"This is different." She stood in the soft, filtered

light coming into the window. She looked delicate. Angelic.

Colby bridged the space she'd placed between them when her assistant had come in. "Why is it?"

Shrugging, she wrinkled her nose. "He's not playing fair."

"What do you mean?"

"We all start out hoping for the best when we get involved with someone."

She made more sense than he expected. When he'd been with Diana he'd been so sure they were right for each other. And they'd been so wrong. "What's different with them?"

As she shook her head, he watched the sway of her earrings. Dangling, gold, they resembled tiny lizards. "I can't say."

Had she really felt something? "Will you tell her?"

"No, I won't."

"Why not? If you could save her from getting hurt by him, why won't you tell her?"

"Because she didn't ask me to find out for her." In a small show of nerves, she looked down, fiddled with the hem of her black blouse, smoothed it over the waistband of her jeans. "I didn't mean to intrude on her privacy."

"Is that a rule you have?" He prided himself on being intelligent, but she confused him as much as she intrigued him. "You said that she's a friend of yours. Won't you do anything to warn her?"

She raised her chin a notch. "I'll try as a friend.

A friend would tell her to get to know him well, find out about his family, where he's from," she said, offering such a reasonable explanation that Colby was more baffled. "Either he won't want to tell her. Or he'll lie. And he'll trip up on a lie."

"Why aren't you suggesting that she read tarot cards or gaze in one of those crystals?"

"That wouldn't work. She'd only believe what she wants." She moved behind a counter and picked up a paper. "I don't want to see her hurt."

She was trying too hard to look relaxed. Colby didn't buy it. She wore the same tight expression when she'd opened the florist's box and seen the dead flowers. Again, she was laboring to hang on to a smile.

When she ambled toward the storeroom, he followed. In the middle of the room, she stopped, and for a second, she stared at the back door. "Was the fellow with you at Joe's Bar a good friend of yours? The dark-haired cowboy with the sneakers?"

"Garrett Hudson." Colby scanned the door. What was wrong with it? "He's been as close as a brother could be."

She turned an interested look on him. "Have you known him long?"

"Since I was five. We met in kindergarten."

"That's so great. And you've been friends ever since?"

"We had a mutual interest. We both liked bugs."

She laughed, but the sparkle wasn't in her eyes. "Quite a common interest."

Feeling concerned for her, he leaned against the closest counter. He wasn't leaving until he learned what was wrong. "It worked for us. We were both from ranches, both as comfortable on a horse as most kids were on bicycles."

"How wonderful to have such a relationship." She perched on the edge of her desk. "Did you go to high school together, too?"

"We both barely finished. I wanted out, I wanted to go on the rodeo circuit. At sixteen I was hooked. I was in junior rodeo, won a few events, but no one took me serious. They all had trouble with this kid who went everywhere on his Harley."

"Hardly the cowboy image."

"They changed their minds when I got on my horse. I kept winning, and no one doubted me then."

"And the motorcycle?"

"I sold it. I couldn't pull a horse trailer with it."

"Ah, the action of a sensible man."

He eyed the open box with the brown flowers. Had something else happened? He was tempted to pull her close, give her some kind of assurance that would explain why she received dead flowers, but he doubted she'd believe the florist had screwed up on the order and delivered the flowers too late. "Who do you think sent the weeds? Leone?"

She directed a frown at him. "I'm surprised that you'd make such an accusation. Do you think she would?"

"Not really," he admitted. "Leone Burton is more

direct. If she doesn't like something, she says so. What was her problem earlier?''

"I'm causing all this hot weather."

He laughed, brushing the comment aside as silly. "Right."

"Really." Her lips curved in a half smile, a sad one. "She's certain I'm responsible for the heat."

Colby shook his head. She was having a laugh at his expense. There was no way Leone Burton would believe that. She was too intelligent to make such a dumb assumption. "What's the real problem between you two?"

"I wish I knew." As if to banish the unpleasant moment from her day, she ceremoniously dumped the flowers in the trash receptacle behind the counter.

Colby sidled closer. He was taunting himself. He could feel the heat of her body. He smelled her scent. It drifted over him, making him remember the kiss. He needed to find out what was wrong, but she smelled like fresh wildflowers. She enticed.

To his satisfaction, she sighed when he kissed the curve of her ear. "Colby, you're making nothing easy."

"Sounds fair. You haven't made it easy for me."

Her body softened against him. "I can't do this."

He couldn't say what clued him in. But he knew she wasn't being coy or playing hard to get. "There's more wrong, isn't there?"

She heaved a breath as if something too weighty was resting on her shoulders. "Yes." In the manner of someone about to face her executioner, she slipped out of his embrace and led the way to the back door. Not saying anything, she opened it wide.

Colby stepped forward. Tacked to the back door was a white sheet of paper. He eyed the simple note. It contained four six-inch-high letters.

M.Y.O.B.

Chapter Five

"Dammit!" Colby swung a look at her. She hugged herself and stood away from the door as if it were booby-trapped. Was she scared? This was all his fault. He'd been too public about contacting her, getting her help. He'd alerted Harriet's killer. While he had doubts about her gift, someone believed Tessa might see the killing.

From the moment Colby had heard about her, he'd scoffed at the idea of her being a visionary. He figured any success rate she had was because she had a knack for guessing. But personal feelings were mingling with his logic, and while he had doubts about her, he was convinced that she believed in her ability to conjure up images of what wasn't visible. "When did this happen?"

"I think while Leone was here. I heard a noise then, but couldn't check it out, so I don't know who did it."

"It's good you left the note on the door."

"I was going to call the sheriff." She reached for the note. "But there's no reason—"

"Leave it!" He grabbed her shoulders, made her face him. "You need to step back from this."

He expected her to agree. She didn't. "I can't do that."

"Why can't you?"

"For the same reason you can't. Though your mother hides her grief, I felt it. It travels on her every breath."

He wanted to hold her. She didn't deserve trouble from anyone. He didn't have to know her for a long time to sense that this woman with her generous heart could be hurt easily.

"She needs to know who killed her sister. She needs closure."

He'd been willing to see a psychic for the same reasons. The authorities had hit a dead end. He'd been willing to try anything, even a clairvoyant, for his mother's sake. "Leone Burton wouldn't do this."

"No, she wouldn't." No uncertainty colored her voice. "I'd never think of her as the culprit. She might see me as the wrong kind, but I view her as classy, too cultured for such antics."

Magnanimous. He doubted he'd have such kind

thoughts about someone hell-bent on destroying his livelihood. "Why aren't you scared?"

"Aren't I?"

Colby didn't respond to her smile. "You need to tell Sheriff Reingard about this note."

"I thought so, too. But what can he do about it? I'm not being threatened, not really. No one broke in."

He wouldn't play along with her so reasonable, so calm act. "How would you know, since you don't have a lock? Tessa, you need to report this."

"I will." She tore the note off the door, then closed it. "I'll be all right now."

Clearly she didn't want to lean on him, on anyone, too much. He wondered who'd taught her that lesson.

The bell above the door rang, and three middle-aged women all talking at the same time ambled in.

When Tessa started forward to greet the women, he spoke to her back. "Call the sheriff," he insisted. In passing, he let his fingers brush her hand. She glanced from him to the women. "And call if you need me."

Colby cursed his stupidity later. He should have asked her out to dinner. At eight that evening, he stood in his kitchen and stirred the spaghetti sauce in the pot on his stove. He wanted to spend more time with her, get to know her. He couldn't say why. They belonged to different worlds. Hell, he ran hot and cold about her. One moment he thought that she might have the sixth sense, and the next moment, a pragmatic streak within him resisted clairvoyance. All he knew with certainty was that he wanted to be with her.

"Smells great." Garrett lounged in the kitchen doorway. He wouldn't knock. He considered other rooms off-limits, in case Colby had a female guest, but not the kitchen. "What are you cooking?"

"Spaghetti." Colby liked puttering around, chopping vegetables, making an omelette, cooking stew or chili. He didn't cook anything fancy but could put together enough to keep from starving.

"Always liked spaghetti."

"Stay," he said, though Garrett was already sitting at the table. Colby grabbed another plate and napkin, then opened a drawer for silverware and stretched to set them on the table.

"That stud horse is working out fine." Garrett removed his hat and dropped it onto an adjacent chair. "I've got two foals coming in."

"Good." Colby spooned the sauce into a bowl. He hadn't had the same success with his mare. Wasn't it Tessa who'd said Ladyfair was pregnant? So much for psychic powers.

"Hey! Should I go on talking to myself or do you want to join in?"

Colby snapped himself from private thoughts. Setting the bowl on the table, he straddled a chair across from Garrett. He'd rather be staring at the lovely Tessa Madison.

"Are you making any progress in finding out who your aunt was seeing?"

Colby spooned sauce over the spaghetti noodles. "None."

"What about the psychic?"

He shrugged, not willing to discuss Tessa, and tore a portion of bread from a long, crusty loaf. "She hasn't been much help."

"You didn't think she would be, if I remember right. But who cares? Right? She's great to look at."

"She hasn't given me any new information." His friend was quiet, too quiet. With no choice, Colby looked up. "Go ahead. What do you want to say?"

Not bashful, Garrett prodded. "Are you seeing her now?"

"Why would you think I am?"

"You went home with her from Joe's Bar the other night." He hunched forward, setting forearms on the table. "You saw her today." A trace of humor slid into his voice. "Be careful, or Moms," he said, using his nickname for Colby's mother, "will be planning the wedding."

No wedding, Colby thought firmly. He'd nearly gotten married once. Once was enough. He no longer was sure he wanted to make that commitment to any woman. "Come on. Grab your plate. There's a game on."

By the fifth inning, Garrett had finished dinner and was devouring a bowl of popcorn.

Leaving him in the study, Colby returned to the kitchen to check his mail. He tossed two bills and an advertising flyer from a Whitehorn supermarket on the counter. With half an ear, he listened to the baseball game while he punched the phone number for Harriet's Boston neighbor. Harriet had kept to herself in Rumor. He doubted she'd acted differently while living in Boston. She'd been an aloof, distant woman who was slow to make friends. Still, he hoped this neighbor had penetrated Harriet's steely demeanor.

Typical of his day, he hit another dead end. No one answered his call. Cussing, he swung around in time to see the team's star pitcher strike out three in a row.

''You're missing a good game,'' Garrett informed him between mouthfuls of popcorn.

What he was really missing was a certain woman. He moseyed away from Garrett and the distraction of the television to step onto the back porch. He wanted to call Tessa. He wanted to hear her voice. The thought sounded dumb even to him. He wasn't easily infatuated or smitten. When he'd been on the rodeo circuit, he used to laugh when he heard about a guy acting stupid about a woman. Colby liked women, respected them. But he didn't believe in acting the fool about one.

Tessa stood on the back porch, let the hot breeze blow through her hair. Closing her eyes, she tried to empty her mind, hoped for an image. Nothing.

She shivered with a chill, though perspiration drenched her back. She was more scared than she wanted to admit to anyone. She'd never been threatened before. In less than twenty-four hours, someone had followed her, phoned her and left her fretting over a silence, sent her dead flowers, and now this message to mind her own business. Someone wanted her to stop. But who? Why couldn't she see the person?

She moved toward a step, then pulled back with the sound of the ringing phone. Before she allowed even a trace of panic to grab hold, praying she'd hear a voice, she lunged for the receiver and offered a sharp hello.

"What are you doing?"

Tessa clutched the phone tighter with the sound of Colby's voice. Her life was suddenly so complicated, she realized as her heart fluttered. "Colby?"

"Hi." He was silent for a moment as if deciding on his words. "I wanted to hear your voice."

She sank to the closest chair. Never would she have expected such a greeting from him. What little resistance she had to him melted. He made her feel. Everything. With a look, he warmed her blood. He made her want to believe that she could have more. That was so ridiculous. Too much of a romantic. She'd always been too much of a romantic. *Protect yourself, shelter your heart,* her mother used to say. She struggled not to make too much of an admittance that might have been lightly said. "Did you think of something else to tell me?"

"Yeah, I miss you."

Her heart hammered as pleasure rushed through her. She closed her eyes, let the softness of his voice float over her. She was more thrilled than she wanted to be, and so afraid to make too much of what he'd said. "Colby—"

"You've got that sound in your voice. It must be

a female thing.'' Laughter warmed his voice. ''My mother gets the same sound when she's exasperated with me.''

He had no idea what getting involved with her might mean to him. ''For good reason, probably,'' she teased, and attempted to steer the conversation away from him. ''Did you find out more about Harriet?''

''I didn't call about that.''

''But you know more, don't you?''

''No. I called Harriet's neighbor,'' he said more seriously. ''She wasn't home. I'll call again tomorrow.''

Tessa pushed open the screen door and stepped onto the back porch again. ''What are you hoping to learn?''

''If she knows anything about my aunt's marriage to Parrish. Like why they were estranged.''

Tessa settled on the top step and stared at the darkness behind her house. ''And you'll ask if she knew anything about Harriet's lover.''

''Right. What were you doing?''

''Sitting outside on the porch.''

''You shouldn't.''

She'd never been skittish about being alone, but she peered hard at the inky darkness. ''I'm all right,'' she insisted even as she wandered into the house. She wished now she had the lock fixed. For good measure, she pushed the back of a chair under the doorknob, then climbed the servant's staircase to her rooms on the second floor.

''Go inside.''

"I did." Feeling hot, she stopped by an end table in her living room to stand in front of a fan. She had to remember what wasn't possible for her. Like her mother, she'd never expect promises from any man.

"I'm attracted to you, Tessa."

She heard the smile in his voice. "I'm attracted to you, too, but—"

"I think you're a beautiful woman."

His voice curled around her like a caress. "Colby—"

"Just say thank you."

She couldn't help smiling. "Thank you. Good night, Colby."

"Tessa?"

"What?"

"Think of me."

A second later, she was listening to the dial tone. Oh, he was dangerous. He made her believe she could have more. She set down the receiver and shook her head. She had to be careful. Very careful.

Colby believed that a good night's sleep was all he needed to get his head on straight. The sensible side of him, which had led him to leave rodeo before he injured himself beyond repair, knew he didn't belong with her. There were other women he was better suited for. They didn't believe in staring at crystals and looking for colored clouds. They wouldn't even consider tofu pizza. They also didn't heat his gut.

Colby awakened by daybreak from a dream of a woman with raven-colored hair and haunting gray eyes, a woman he wanted to make love with. Annoyed with himself, he had breakfast and forced himself to stay at the ranch and do the one job he hated. He spent the morning closeted with his computer and record keeping.

By afternoon, only when he was finished did he let himself leave the study. He was congratulating himself for resisting the temptation to go see her when the phone rang.

His mother rushed words. "Warren Parrish is at Harriet's house," she said instead of a greeting. "Someone saw him there yesterday, too."

"I'll meet you there at three."

"I'm sorry to bother you," his mother said, not for the first time, when Colby was climbing out of his truck half an hour later.

With her, he walked toward his aunt's house, a white bungalow with yellow shutters and a giant willow in the front yard. The house had been sealed by authorities, but Parrish stood on the porch as if he owned the place. "Has he been here all day?" Colby asked his mother.

"Yes, I believe he has. I needed reinforcements or I wouldn't have asked you to meet me." Disgust edged her voice. "He views me as the little woman."

Colby masked a grin but found humor in her words. His mother definitely was not the little woman. Though she was slim, delicate-looking, she had never let anyone back her down when she thought she was right.

"Your father had to drive to Billings for a truck part or he'd be with me."

"No problem, Mom." Colby figured Parrish needed to know that all of the Holmes family planned to keep an eye on him.

"I can't believe he's still here," she said about Parrish.

Beneath his hand under her arm, Colby felt her fury.

For the first time since Colby had met Parrish, he wasn't smoking one of his cigars. "Hello, Louise. Colby. What are you doing here?"

"That's my question," Louise said.

"I have every right to be here." Parrish delivered a slow, amused smile. "I was Harriet's husband. This will be mine soon. So don't think of touching anything that belonged to her."

"Nothing! You will get nothing," Colby's mother yelled. "If you break in there, we'll press charges."

Colby wasn't certain she legally had that right. "Mom, let's go." He could have forced a confrontation, but that would only upset his mother more. "He can't get in. Can't do anything. When we have answers, we won't have to put up with him," he said to soothe her while they walked to his truck.

He drove her home and made the call to Harriet's neighbor in Boston again. The conversation was brief, leaving them with more questions than answers.

Colby left her and drove to town to see the sheriff.

"He's not here right now," Holt informed him after a greeting was exchanged.

He'd rather talk to Holt, anyway. Though they'd clashed a few times at the beginning of the investigation, they respected each other. "This is about what we discussed." Colby relayed the information he planned to share with Tessa and told Holt about Parrish hanging out at Harriet's house.

"I'll ride by." Holt swiveled his chair away and set papers on a counter behind him. "And I'll fill the sheriff in about what you've learned. Where are you headed now?"

"To Tessa's. My mother found more photos to show her."

Holt shrugged in a noncommittal way as if not wanting to voice an opinion about Tessa's power.

"Did Tessa tell you what happened at her store?"

Holt's frown deepened as Colby told him about the M.Y.O.B. message. "I sure don't like the sound of that. I think it would be a good idea to keep an eye on Mystic Treasures."

Satisfied with his response, Colby left. He stalled on the sidewalk and withdrew the photos from his shirt pocket. One was of Harriet standing in front of a tiger's cage at a zoo. She was smiling, appearing so different from the way Colby had seen her most of the time. "Who were you?" Colby said aloud to the woman in the picture.

"Talking to yourself now, Colby?"

Looking up, he was met by the smile of a leggy redhead. Diana stood beside a bright red sports car. He expected a slight pang. She looked as beautiful as ever, but he felt nothing. He'd been engaged to the woman smiling at him. He should have felt something.

"I heard you were back in Rumor," he said, closing the space between them. The moment wouldn't be easy, he realized in that instant. "I'm sorry about your husband." If he learned anything from the engagement to Diana, it was that he'd had one shot at a permanent relationship with a woman and didn't want another.

"It was unexpected." She held out a ringless left hand. "I never thought I'd be such a young widow. But we both know that marriage was a mistake."

"Was it?"

She drew a tight breath and smiled. "Yes. That's why I'm back. I came to see you."

Tessa stood at the window of Mystic Treasures. To stir interest, she'd removed the crystal display and propped a zodiac chart in the window. Along with it, she draped an assortment of amulets over a ruby-red velvet display stand.

From the bay window she saw Colby and the woman standing near him. So that was Diana? Tall, polished, sexy. Diana touched his arm, leaned close. She wanted him back. Tessa didn't need to hear their conversation to know that. Telltale movements carried a clear meaning. Did he still love her? Tessa wondered.

She watched a moment longer, expecting Diana Lynscot to bat eyelashes at him. A mass of coppery-colored hair blew in the warm breeze. She looked like a Miss America contestant.

According to Marla, they'd broken off the engagement because Colby traveled so much on the rodeo circuit and couldn't give Diana the home life she wanted, so she married another. Older than her, her new husband had recently died. But now, retired from rodeo, Colby could give Diana that stable life. Possibly they both wanted to resume their relationship.

People accepted Diana. Born and raised in a neighboring town, she was part of the community, was perfect for him. If she and Colby got back together, people would nod approvingly, say something like, "They were destined for each other."

They'd say just the opposite if he were with Tessa.

"Do you daydream a lot?"

Lost in thought, she hadn't even heard the bell ring. Turning, she practically stood in Colby's embrace. Before she had time to think, he framed her face with his hands and gave her a long, lingering kiss.

Stunned. There was no other word to describe what she was feeling. *Don't take my breath away.* She needed to remember that there was another woman.

"Isn't it time to close for the day?"

"Almost."

"Good. Then have dinner with me. And before you say, Colby—"

She tried for her best I'm-not-amused look. As he chuckled, she knew she'd failed. It was natural that this attraction existed. He was macho, possessed an enormous amount of charm, of sexuality. Perhaps she needed to spend time with him. She needed him to realize she wasn't someone to date on a whim, someone to amuse him, or worse, she wasn't someone to make his ex-fiancée jealous. "Were you a tease as a little boy, too?"

"Terrible one." He fiddled with a strand of hair near her ear. "Look, I have to eat and so do you. Let's do it together. If it will make you feel better, we'll discuss the business of Warren Parrish."

"Have you learned more?"

"Food first?"

"All right." Nerves hummed with his nearness. "Food first." When had she felt so weak with a man? she wondered.

"Why didn't you tell the sheriff about what happened last night at the store?" Colby asked once they were seated at the table in the Rooftop Café.

She'd planned to, but a sheriff's report meant making her problems public, and she was trying so hard to keep a low profile. "If I did, others might hear about what happened."

"Secrets are hard to keep in this town." He motioned at the menu in her hands. "What do you like?"

"Everything."

"No one likes everything," he said, running a finger across the top of her hand.

A thrill that seemed unbelievably adolescent skittered through her. "I do." She had to get a grip on this.

"Brussels sprouts?"

"Yes." Tessa made herself look up, meet his eyes. They gentled a face that bore a hard, stubborn look. She viewed his stubbornness as a good trait. She admired people who didn't give up. A lesson learned from one man who'd run when life got too difficult.

"Sauerkraut?"

Tessa couldn't help laughing. "Yes."

"Cauliflower?"

What was the point to the twenty questions? "I gather you don't like those foods."

He looked pained. Easily she imagined him making the same face twenty years ago. *What did you do for fun as a boy? What's your favorite pie? What Christmas present did you long for most?* She wanted to ask. "Do you like opera?"

He slitted his eyes at her. "Do you?"

"Certain ones." As the server appeared at their table, she looked away from the amusement in his eyes and quickly scanned the menu. She ordered a chicken salad, then waited until they were alone before asking, "Tell me now what you've learned about Harriet when she was in Boston."

A frown knitted his brow. "Look at these first." He set photographs on the table close to her. "My mom found these. Harriet was in Boston when they were taken."

Tessa reached for one photo. "I don't know if I'll feel anything." The tip of a finger touched one corner of the top photograph.

"Don't leave." A gut-wrenching ache hit Tessa before she could block it. *Tears smarted in her eyes.*

Her stomach clenched. "You can't leave," she yelled at his back, watching him storm toward the door. "I love you." When he slammed the door, she jumped. Though she squeezed her eyes tight, she felt the tears on her cheeks. An ache rising within her, she touched her belly. "How could you leave me?" Shame. It filled her. She'd begged him not to leave. She'd never thought she'd beg anyone.

"Tessa." Colby's voice broke in on the image. "What's wrong?"

She placed a hand on her chest in response to an empty sensation in the vicinity of her heart. "She cried so hard. Hurt so much."

"Who?"

"Harriet. He hurt her." She stared at the hand that he'd closed over hers. "It was her lover." No one had ever touched her, offered comfort after she'd had a vision. Most people backed away instead of coming closer. She shook her head. "I'm sorry. I don't know who it was." She didn't want to let Harriet's feelings take over her body again. There was too much hurt.

She sat back, aware people were staring at them. "Someone hurt her." More than that. She knew Harriet had kept her pain tight within, shared it with no one. "Will you tell me now what you learned from the neighbor?" she asked, in need of a distraction after such intense feelings.

He leveled a frown at the steaming black coffee in his cup. "Unfortunately the marriage wasn't wonderful. According to the neighbor, Harriet caught Warren with another woman on their wedding night."

Tessa imagined Harriet's heartbreak at such a betrayal. She'd waited so long to find someone to love, and to be loved. Then when she'd finally thought she'd found someone, he'd been unfaithful to her immediately. "Why? Why did he do that to her?"

"He married her for her money."

"Oh, Colby, that is so sad. Terribly sad."

"That might be what you were seeing." He inclined his head, forcing eye contact. "What do you think?"

"I don't know." She stayed silent as the server set their plates before them.

"According to Harriet's neighbor, Harriet fled that night," Colby said, once they were alone and eating. "That's when she came back to Rumor. The woman said no one in Boston had known where she'd gone until almost a year later."

How difficult it would be for him to be around Parrish. "I'm sorry."

He looked up from the steak on his plate, sent her a puzzled frown. "About what?"

"I know how you feel about Warren Parrish. I'm sorry you have to deal with him."

He gave her an unconvincing grin. "Can't you see into the future for me? Tell me how long I have to put up with him?"

Tessa wasn't offended. She'd heard the same request often enough from others. "No, I can't do that."

He cut his steak. "If you don't want to tell the future, then tell me about your past."

She poked a fork into her chicken salad. "You'll be bored."

"Hardly."

Too easily he could make her a believer. How ironic that was. He wouldn't believe in her power, but he had the ability to make her want to consider love again. "What did you want to be when you grew up?"

He didn't hesitate. "A cowboy."

She laughed and speared a lettuce leaf. "How many men can say they got their wish?"

"Lucky man, I guess," he said about himself, but she knew how much he'd sacrificed physically and emotionally to attain goals in rodeo. His many injuries and his broken engagement to Diana came to mind. She'd also heard how hard he worked on his ranch since settling down. Before Harriet had died, he'd devoted all his time to the ranch, never came to town. She remembered the warm hellos from the customers at Joe's Bar who were glad to see him.

"When you were growing up, where did you live? Chicago?"

"No. We moved a lot. The Poconos. Las Vegas. Anywhere there was a resort. My mother worked as a seer at a lot of high-priced resorts, telling fortunes. Madam Cassandra."

"An unusual childhood?"

"I thought it was normal." Before she was nine, she'd hated leaving friends. There hadn't been many after parents learned about her visions.

"My mom said that yours wanted to travel."

Tessa didn't correct him. She knew that was what everyone thought.

"Was one of those a favorite place?"

"A resort in New Hampshire. We lived on the premises in a caretaker's cottage. We had a house for a while, and a flower garden." She hadn't meant to say more, but the memory was such a good one. "I'd sneak into the kitchen and get delicious desserts. I have an insatiable sweet tooth. I'll eat lemon meringue pie for breakfast." His wince stirred her laugh. "Anyway, after school, I'd spend hours in the kitchen, watching the cook. She'd make some wonderful desserts." She'd been grateful for that woman's kindness and friendship. At twelve, it hadn't been easy for her to make friends.

"A good time?"

"My mother was a fun person," she said honestly. "We had a good life." A different one, by his standards. She looked away, realized they were being watched by other diners. She guessed people were gossiping about them. Why would one of their own choose to be with the spacey owner of that weird shop?

"Was there anything you wanted?"

A home, a place to call my own. "Everyone yearns for something. Don't you?"

"That's a loaded question." He moved his thumb, caressing the top of her hand. The gesture was loverlike, intimate. "To be with you."

She didn't think he was the kind of man who'd use

a woman, but she remembered how close he'd stood to Diana. How well did she know him? "Why?"

His eyes held hers. "Someone hurt you badly, didn't he?"

"I'm not looking for more in my life right now." Was she intriguing to him because she was different? Or was he using her to forget another? *I don't want to be hurt again.* "I'm not looking for promises."

"Neither am I."

Chapter Six

Colby had read such sadness in her eyes that he'd deliberately made himself back off. Despite her smile earlier, when she'd let it slip that friendships hadn't been easy, he'd sensed a life filled with disappointments.

Because she'd made it clear that she wanted space, he'd planned to give her a few days. The act was a selfish one. He thought if he stayed away from her, he'd stop thinking so much about her. The plan failed.

By eight-thirty the next morning, twice he caught himself remembering the warning about the cowboy on his lap, and he had to give himself a mental kick. Never gullible or easily fooled, he hit the computer in his office and did some morning research about parapsychologists and ESP and telepathy. He'd yet to ask Tessa about claims people made that she was a scryer and could crystal gaze. Tarot cards, crystals, runes, palmistry all belonged in a different world.

He believed in what he could see, taste, feel. He wasn't impressionable or superstitious. He refused to think too much about the past. He believed in concentrating on now, not the future.

At this moment, on this sunny day, he wanted to see Tessa. That probably wasn't the most rational decision he'd made, but sometimes a person went with gut instinct.

At first, he'd been curious about her. He wondered if that was because she was so different. People claimed she was strange. The thought annoyed him. There was nothing peculiar about her. She walked to the beat of her own drummer, took her own counsel, believed in things he didn't understand, but that didn't make her odd. And he knew then that more than desire led him. Softer, gentler feelings existed for her.

By ten o'clock, he strolled into Mystic Treasures, determined to be with her. He recalled the last time he'd felt like this. He'd been sixteen with hormones raging for Leah Trecker, a sexy little blonde who wore the shortest skirts in the county. Like then, he had no choice. But unlike then, he wouldn't stand at her door looking like a grinning fool. Before he stepped into the store, he'd drummed up a legitimate reason for being there. Making a fool of himself over any female wasn't something he'd ever do again.

Tessa stood near a display of crystal balls. In the soft light filtering into the room from the octagonal window, she was cast in an ethereal glow. He skimmed the slim body that was more angles than curves. Blue, ankle-length, the dress had tiny white flowers. On her feet were those sandals he viewed as a flimsy excuse for shoes.

He closed the door behind him but stayed by it until she looked up. He wanted to see if she'd react to him. He wasn't disappointed. For an instant, he swore she looked pleased to see him, but if he'd blinked, he'd have never seen it. She was good at hiding feelings, he realized. It might take time to catch on to nuances, to understand what a tilt of her head or a shrug of a shoulder or a subtle turn of her body meant. "I brought a bribe." He moved near, caught her scent. The fragrance curled around him like a seductive cocoon. "I brought you breakfast," he said, setting a bag from the Calico Diner on the counter.

Because the sight of him had quickened her heartbeat, Tessa pretended interest in the bag's contents. Even before he removed a plastic cup, she smelled the rich aroma of the coffee. "What else do you have in there?" Suddenly impatient, she peered into the bag. "Croissants?" She was intrigued. She couldn't mask her astonishment. "You look more like a biscuits and gravy man."

He took off his hat and set it, too, on the counter. "I like them." His head bent close to hers as he reached into the bag. "There's more in there."

She peered into the bag and smiled. "You're a bad influence."

"One serving of lemon meringue pie for the lady with the sweet tooth."

She laughed. She hadn't wanted to be amused. Certainly she didn't want to be charmed. But she had little choice. "Did you bring two forks?"

"I'll pass." His hand touched hers. There it was again, the warm, secure sensation she'd felt the first time he touched her. *Oh, say it like it is.* A rightness descended on her whenever he was near. She wished—she wished her mother was alive, that she had someone to talk to about what she felt whenever he touched her. "You don't know how to live," she teased to stop her serious ponderings about him.

"Die happy," he said on a laugh before he took a bite of his croissant.

"So what is it you're trying to bribe me to do?"

"Parrish plans to hang around to find out if he inherited anything." A trace of frustration colored his voice. "We have to do something, get answers. Will you go to the library with me?"

His request made sense. Outside of her home, Harriet had spent most of her time at the library. "If I go there with you, then I might feel something?"

"That's possible."

On a Saturday afternoon, the library was quiet but not empty. Lacking an abundance of windows, the two-story, redbrick building was huge but dark inside with mostly artificial lights. Tessa walked down an aisle between large tables where students from the local high school were studying.

With Colby, she sat at one of the varnished pine tables. She tried not to think about Harriet, to clear her mind of pressure. She made small talk with Colby about how nice the library was for a small town.

"Their pride and joy, my mother says."

To not disturb others, she spoke low. "Louise came into the store this morning. She bought a love amulet."

Colby removed his hat. "My next birthday present, no doubt. My mother is looking for a wife."

"Your mother is?"

"Of course." A slow smile lit his face. "She doesn't think I'm capable."

"Or have an inclination to?" Tessa asked. If he wanted to find someone, he wouldn't have a difficult time. She couldn't help wondering if he still pined for Diana, if that kept him from being satisfied with anyone else. She wasn't sure how much he'd be willing to discuss. "I heard about your broken engagement. I'm sorry."

He sent her a curious look. "Why?"

"It must be a painful memory."

"We called it quits a month before the wedding." That he didn't offer more made Tessa stay silent. "Now my mother feels I might dodge matrimony."

Was that because he was marriage shy or still in love with the ex-fiancée? If that was true, she couldn't fault Louise for being concerned. "Does it upset you that she's trying to play matchmaker?"

"I humor her."

She heard such fondness. "You get along well?"

"Really well. My parents made a good life for me. They doted on me." His smile widened. "Although they briefly threatened to disown me if I went into rodeo."

"They didn't want you to?"

"She's a mom. She was afraid I'd get hurt."

"And you did. Often."

"Still they came to every rodeo within a day's drive of Rumor to cheer me on."

How difficult it must have been to deal with a son who sought thrills, first on a motorcycle and then on an angry, bucking Brahman. "And now they want you to get married."

"What she really wants is a grandchild. Do you see one in my future?"

By his teasing manner, he showed he still didn't believe in what she could do. "I don't predict. Remember?"

He released a chuckle and received a shh from Molly Brewster, the librarian in charge since Harriet's death.

Tessa wondered why the quiet, subtle beauty pulled lovely blond hair tightly back in a twist. She offered Molly a quick smile, received a faint one from her. Though only in her late twenties, Molly looked weary. *She doesn't trust easily,* Tessa guessed, but didn't allow herself to delve deeper, to learn what secret Molly kept close.

"Hello, Colby."

Tessa looked up with him in response to Dee Dee Reingard's hello. The sheriff's wife, Dee Dee was the doting mother of five, and at fifty, hardly the person to have something in common with an ex-rodeo ladies' man. "I don't know her," Tessa said when Dee Dee moved on to check out an armful of children's books.

"I know Dave," he said about the town's sheriff, "better than her, but I guess he put her onto me. They have a pack of kids."

"I'd heard. Is that how you know her? Because of her kids?"

"That's our connection. She's into PTA, always at all of her kids' games. When I came back to town, she pounced on me to coach one of the teams."

"Did you agree?"

He delivered a crooked grin so full of boyish charm that Tessa's heart turned. "What do I know about soccer?" he said.

"What about baseball?"

"I played a little. Enough to break a few school windows."

How different they'd been as children. She glanced around at the aisles of books. As a child, she'd loved to read, escaped into worlds different from her own. She'd been quiet, even a touch shy. She doubted either of those words would have described Colby as a child. "Were you always getting in trouble?"

"Never." He chuckled low, got another shh from a frowning Molly. "She's almost as conscientious as a librarian we had in school. She used to shh if one of the kids sneezed."

Tessa brought herself to why they were really together, why they were in the library. "Do you think Harriet was like that?"

"Molly had to learn it somewhere. My aunt came across as stiff. She wasn't like my mother. You know how she is." Unexpectedly his fingers skimmed the nape of her neck. "She'll talk to a tree. Harriet was the opposite. When I was home, she didn't seem too interested in getting together. I don't push."

Tessa cast a glance around, saw eyes widen because he was touching her and drew back to place distance between them. "You don't?" She already knew he had a relentless streak. "I didn't think you ever take no for an answer."

"It's one of my irresistible flaws."

She couldn't help it—she laughed. Heads swung toward her. Tessa slammed a hand over her mouth and fought not to giggle harder. "We're going to get kicked out," she whispered, louder than she intended. She hadn't meant to sit so long with him, but he effortlessly did something that no other man had—he made her feel comfortable. He made her forget she was different. She pushed back her chair. "I'd better get busy."

Inching her way down an aisle, she touched the spines of several books about crafts before moving to the aisle containing books about art and music.

"Can I talk or will that bother you?" Colby asked, standing behind her.

She whispered, "You can talk."

He peered over her shoulder. "It makes sense that she touched every book in here."

She took another second, then looked at him. "That's what I thought." *Many hands appeared.* Resisting any response to them, Tessa moved on. The fiction section stretched along a side and back wall. She wandered along, touched the books by Austen, Brontë, Caldwell, Fitzgerald, Hemingway, Michener, Steinbeck. Nothing. "What did she like to read? Do you know?"

Colby stopped with her in front of books about calligraphy. "She was a history buff. My mom sent her a book about Gettysburg."

She looked past him, saw the heads of two elderly women angled close with their whispering. "Let's go upstairs then." For privacy, teenagers gathered at the tables on the second floor. The couples were more interested in each other than anyone else.

Tessa spent a few minutes running fingertips over several Civil War publications. Remembering Colby's words, she pulled out a large gray book filled with pages of photographs of officers and soldiers who'd served under Grant and Lee. So many feelings. Too many faces. She couldn't focus. "This isn't going well, Colby."

"Hey, it was a thought. Why don't we try Harriet's desk," he suggested.

Together, they descended the stairs and headed toward the small office in a corner of the room. "Go in," Colby said. "I'll talk to Molly about us checking the desk." Tessa was moving behind the large oak desk when he came in.

"It's okay with her."

Tessa nudged back the chair and opened a drawer. Rubber bands, paper clips, tacks were compartmentalized in a plastic tray. Pencils all of the same length were lined up in one slot of the pencil container. The other held pens. Harriet had been neat, almost obsessively so, Tessa thought, noticing that Harriet had grouped the tacks by colors. Tessa had hoped that touching Harriet's things would trigger her to see something Harriet had experienced. "I'm getting nothing."

"Sit in her chair."

Tessa started to protest. "I can't do that. People will be upset."

"Sit." Gently he pressed a hand on her shoulder.

Sitting, she waited to feel a sense of the woman who used the chair every day for years. No feeling came. Why? Why was she being blocked? Looking down, Tessa saw a pen, a gold-plated one, and picked it up. The word *Harriet* was inscribed on it in cursive lettering. Had a friend, someone close given it to her? A colleague would have chosen the full name, Harriet Martel, and...

She unpinned her hair, let it hang loose, drape her shoulders. Smiling, she reached out with bare arms to the man bending over her. She didn't want to wait. Hurry, she wanted to yell. She pulled him down to her, felt his heat, the hardness of him against her. Callused, his hand moved up her ribs, cupped her breast. More heat. His mouth now. On her nipple, drawing it into his mouth, sucking it, lapping at it with his tongue. Sensation sprinted through her. All day she'd waited for him. She couldn't get enough of him. Love me. Please love me. She wouldn't say the words, wouldn't beg him. But she couldn't get enough of him. Take me. Take me. "Take me," she whispered and opened her legs, welcomed the feel of the hard shaft inside her.

Tessa broke away. Her breathing quick, she swallowed against a dry mouth. With fingertips she touched the perspiration above her upper lip. She hadn't wanted to feel more of their passion. She couldn't see his face. All she received was an image of his bare back, of brown hair. "The man who touched this was Harriet's lover," she said, holding out the pen to Colby. "He might have given it to her."

"Her killer? Warren?"

Tessa shook her head. "I don't know," she said, louder than she'd planned, and quickly lowered her voice. "They were making love."

"You saw that?" he asked, looking incredulous.

"And felt it." She avoided looking at him. He didn't believe in a sixth sense or second sight.

"What did he look like?"

She wished she could give him a description. "I don't know. The man was faceless to me. I don't have any clue as to his identity." She sat for another moment. There was something. The desk hid something. But what? She looked down again, studied Harriet's things. There was nothing here. Somewhere else.

The buzz of voices reached her. Tessa looked through the office doorway to the library checkout counter. During the moment too much of Harriet's emotions filled her, she'd drawn attention to herself.

"Want to leave?" Colby questioned.

She stood and pushed in the chair. She was so tired. "Yes. I'm sorry I couldn't give you more." She'd failed just as he'd expected, hadn't she?

Eyes stayed on them as they walked out of the office toward the exit and the double glass doors. He was silent while they strolled toward the store. She could imagine his thoughts. She'd acted odd. It could get worse. If he viewed her as out of step with him after that mild vision, what would he think if she had a full-blown one? Now was as good a time as any to end this. "I'm sorry I haven't been able to help. I warned you that might happen."

"We're not done."

Tessa slowed her stride on the stairs to Mystic Treasures and slanted a look at him.

His hand cupped her elbow, halting her. "We can keep trying."

A stubborn man, she mused, feeling both admiration and annoyance. When did he give up? Maybe he wouldn't until he had answers.

She climbed the rest of the stairs. But before she could step inside, he caught her arm. He stood practically on top of her. It was insane not to move, wasn't it? Of course, it was.

But she remained rooted to the spot, raising her face to his. His eyes darkened before his mouth met hers. Tessa closed her eyes. She didn't need to see.

She felt his smiling lips on her cheek. Pleasure blossomed within her.

She captured to memory the clean, soapy smell of him, the soothing touch of his hand on her hair at the back of her head. Her mind emptied. A pang of longing slithered through her. She slid her hands from his waist to his back while her tongue responded to his.

As he tangled his fingers in her hair, she strained against him to absorb the touch of the body supporting her, the strength, the muscles, the heat of him. The sweet play of his lips, the moist heat of his tongue demanded response and made her every denial sound like a lie. Pliant, willing, she let senses take over. Feel. That's all that mattered. She wanted to be swept away, but what if love came, confused everything?

She struggled to draw back. How could she? Oh, she had to, didn't she? This would never work. How dumb she was. She couldn't keep doing this. Another woman existed. For all she knew, he might still be in love with Diana.

Struggling with herself, she turned her mouth from his, but he held her tightly to him. She didn't resist. She needed his steadiness to muddle her way from the excitement pumping through her. If he kissed her again, every sensible thought she possessed would flee. "Colby." His name was spoken on a ragged breath.

"It's not fair," he said in a voice that sounded rough.

Was it possible she'd made him feel as if the earth had rocked? That's how she'd felt. "What isn't?"

Feather light, he kissed one corner and then the other of her mouth. "How wonderful you taste."

Tessa drew an uneven breath. *You take my breath away.* He made her senseless. What other excuse did she have for standing in the doorway, in the light of the shop for anyone wandering by to see? Fine job she was doing of being inconspicuous. "I have to go in." She gestured over her shoulder and saw a beaming Marla behind the counter.

"Why?"

A quiet challenge stretched between them. "Because I don't know what I want," Tessa said honestly.

With reluctance, he released her. Before she turned, he touched her chin, forced her eyes to meet his. "I do," he said so softly that the words came out whispered. "I want you."

She wanted him, too. He had no idea how much. Tessa hurried inside. No one had ever caused such turmoil in her life before.

A customer, a regular who lived her life by the zodiac and the position of the stars, gave Tessa a knowing grin. Tessa was in no mood to combat Marla or the woman's intentions, which might include singing Colby Holmes's praises. The customer passed, still grinning, and trailed Colby down the stairs. Mentally Tessa moaned. She'd be the number-one topic for the gossips in the morning. "You can leave, Marla."

"Okay," she said too brightly and snatched her oversize shoulder bag from the cabinet behind the counter. "Oh." She stopped at the doorway and pivoted. "I forgot. You got more flowers. The box is on your desk." A speculative smile came to her face. "Someone is trying to make an impression."

Tessa merely smiled. It was better no one knew the flowers weren't being sent as a token of affection. She waited until she was alone before she twisted to look at the long white box. Drawing a deep breath, with dread, she crossed the room. For a long moment she stared at the box, then hurriedly she slid the ribbon off and lifted the lid. Whoever was sending the dead flowers better try something new. This wasn't working anymore. She smashed the lid back on the box.

Suddenly exhausted, she climbed the inside staircase to her second-floor quarters. She was tired, tired of the scare tactics, tired of fighting herself whenever she was with Colby. She couldn't deny that desire crackled in the air between them. She couldn't deny a longing to be with him. But there was so much risk involved.

Filled with uncertainty, she opened the door to her living quarters. She flicked on a light and stepped into the living room. In mid-stride, she froze as panic swept through her.

On an end table was another white florist's box.

Chapter Seven

Colby hadn't been ready to call it a night. A sliver of moon peeked out from behind a fast-moving cloud. They needed rain. Instead the sky lit with lightning. He'd belonged to the volunteer fire department since he'd turned seventeen. Whenever he returned to town from competing, he was on call. That might come any day. The storm season had started a few weeks ago. The woods were dry—zero humidity, high temperatures—danger existed.

He reached his truck but didn't climb in. He needed to think. Nothing made sense to him these days. He wasn't a man easily enchanted. He was the one who usually charmed, but honest to the core, he knew Tessa was inching her way under his skin.

Was that why he was worried about her? By going

to the library, by trying to see something, she'd put herself up for ridicule. He knew a few people who'd say that was her fault. She was the one who made outlandish claims that she could see what wasn't visible.

What had happened today? When she'd held the pen, he'd seen the look of a woman seduced come over her face. Glazed, her eyes had looked beyond him, beyond the walls of Harriet's office. She'd said that she'd seen—felt—Harriet's passion with her lover. Was that really possible?

None of this made sense, not the kind of sense he understood. A day, an hour ago, he wouldn't have believed she'd felt anything, but now protective instincts rose within him. If necessary he'd defend her.

But did he believe her? Damn, he didn't know. Was he really supposed to believe she saw some faceless man? With a look up, he stopped. At some moment, he'd turned, and stood now in front of Mystic Treasures. Tessa had closed the store for the night. A light shone in a second-floor window.

Colby went around the house and climbed the back stairs of the renovated Victorian. From the first landing, he saw the door—open. Uneasiness skittered up his spine. He scaled the steps two at a time, found her standing with her back against a wall. She looked pale, her eyes wide. She looked frightened. "Tessa."

Only her head moved. She stared at him, but a long moment passed before her eyes focused. "Colby." She said his name again when he wrapped his arms around her.

Against his body, her slim one trembled. "What happened?" he asked.

"Someone broke in." She swayed into him, pressed her cheek against his jaw. "Was here."

He felt her shudder. "You aren't hurt?"

"No." But she clung to him as if suddenly weak-kneed. "No one was here."

When he touched her chin, she raised her face to him. "Was anything taken?"

"No. Left," she said in a voice that still sounded shaky. "Something was left." She turned, pointed toward the florist's box. "It's the second one today. Another one came to the store. Then when I came up here, I found that one."

"Did you call the sheriff's office?"

"I didn't. What would I say? Nothing was taken."

"Tessa, that doesn't matter. Call him."

Dave Reingard showed up within a few minutes. "You're sure you weren't hurt?"

"No, I'm not." Tessa tried to relax and leaned back on the beige sofa. Staying in the crook of Colby's arm, she hugged a pumpkin-colored pillow to her chest. She didn't like someone else trying to control her life. In the past, she'd been unwelcome, shunned, ridiculed by some, but never had she been threatened. Most people believed in her or were indifferent to her. Had she done something to scare Harriet's killer? What had she done?

The sheriff seemed to have a similar thought. "Tessa, I know you've been helping Colby."

She tried a smile. But for some reason, she felt annoyed as he bent his head to open a pistachio nut. *Someone's scaring me. Pay attention.* The criticism wasn't fair, but myriad emotions teetered close to the surface.

"Tessa." Colby squeezed a hand on her shoulder. "Dave asked if you'd had any visions about the flowers."

She was ashamed to admit she'd avoided touching the flowers, had blocked images, fearful of what hurtful feelings she might have. "No." When had she become such a coward? she wondered.

"Since there was no actual threat—" Dave shrugged a shoulder. "There isn't much I can do."

Tessa sent Colby an I-told-you-so look.

"I'll write up a report, but I can't do much else." Before leaving them, he offered an assurance that he'd drive by often.

Colby swore as the door shut behind Dave. "Well, there's something we can do."

Tessa rounded a look at him. She'd schooled herself to ignore unpleasant experiences, but this one was different. "This might be the prank of someone who wants my store closed."

He acted deaf. "This isn't safe, Tessa."

He wasn't helping. Hadn't she wrestled with initial shivers of fear ever since she'd walked in, seen the box? "I'm not scared."

"I am for you."

Other than her mother, had anyone ever said anything so caring to her before?

"Come home with me. Stay with me until we know who's doing this."

His offer stunned her.

"Let me be your friend. No strings," he assured.

"I can't change my life."

"You can be careful," he said firmly. "Be careful with me." He grabbed her arms. "At least stay at the ranch with me for a few days until we get locks on these doors." Soothingly he ran his thumbs over her arms. "And let's find out who's doing this."

He'd scared her good this time. She wouldn't have called the sheriff's department if she hadn't been. That's what he'd wanted. She'd stop messing around in what wasn't her business. He couldn't take any chances that she might be able to do some hocus-pocus garbage, might really see him.

Tessa rested her head against the back of the seat and closed her eyes. She listened to the hum of the engine, was aware of each bump in the road. It felt so good to lean on someone after being alone for so many years. She'd always been strong. Hadn't she stood alone at seventeen when her mother had died? She'd been grief-stricken. The one person in the world who'd cared about her, who'd loved her, who'd understood her was gone. After the disappointment with Seth, she'd begun to accept a life alone—until Colby.

"Are you sleeping?"

She opened her eyes as Colby slowed the truck. "Are we at the ranch?"

"We're here."

She wished it was daylight, that she could see more of the place he called home than the silhouettes of trees and a corral fence. As he negotiated the truck onto a gravel drive, she got impressions. Mountains in the distance, outbuildings, a stable, a two-story, light-colored farmhouse surrounded by tall shade-bearing trees. She'd see more in the morning. Stepping out of his truck, she was greeted by the sound of horses and animal smells on the night air.

Her carryall dangling in his hand, Colby rounded the front of the truck. "Come on." He slammed the truck door for her. "You're probably tired."

She had been. Now, curious about this place he called home, she felt less weary. She brushed back hair that was tossed forward by the wind, then climbed the steps to a wide front porch. Before stepping inside, she noted the swing, made a mental plan to sit on it tomorrow.

The living room was masculine, rustic, leather and wood with Western art on the walls. And immaculate. She eyed the big-screen television, the speakers and audio system. He liked his toys.

He gave her a semblance of a grin. "Still skittish?"

"A little." Though the flowers were scare tactics, Tessa sensed the sender's anger when she touched the florist's box. The person who sent them was feeling frustrated, desperate. "It's amazing how a few dead flowers can be so unnerving," she said, trying to make light of everything. But the idea that someone had walked into her home uninvited to leave the flowers churned up nerves.

"That's the plan, probably."

What she detested most of all was the fear, she decided while climbing the oak staircase with him. The person had made her afraid to stay in her own home. Somehow she had to get past that feeling. She'd never considered herself a coward, didn't plan on starting to be one now.

"You need to rest." He opened a door. "Here."

The room was feminine. The wallpaper had tiny blue forget-me-not flowers on a white background. A patchwork quilt mostly done in blues draped the bed with its brass headboard. Nearby on a mahogany dresser was an antique pitcher and bowl, and on an adjacent wall was a small mahogany desk with a brass lamp. "This is so nice. Do you take care of the house yourself?"

He gave her a you've-got-to-be-kidding look before he angled away to set her carryall on an upholstered chair done in the same color blue as the quilt. "You mean do I dust?"

She laughed, because the idea did sound silly. "I guess not."

"No, I guess not. I have a neighbor lady who likes to earn some extra money and comes in once a week to keep the place up. She dusts and vacuums."

Tessa doubted the woman was overworked. The house was straight, incredibly neat. She realized she hadn't expected him to be sloppy. A person with an organized mind didn't usually live in chaos.

"I'm at the end of the hall if you need anything."

She nearly smiled. He was everything she thought she'd never have and everything she'd always wanted.

His fingers skimmed her cheek. "You'll be all right here," he assured her.

Tessa watched the door close behind him. She had no doubt that she'd be safe, but she wasn't sure she'd be all right. *What about heartbreak?* she wanted to ask him.

Facing the shower nozzle, Colby closed his eyes and let the spray rush over his head for a moment before reaching for a towel. Quickly he dried off, then wandered into the bedroom. Every time he looked at her, his gut tightened. Temptation swept through him to touch her—her hand, the slim curve of her neck, her cheek.

He liked the way her hair looked, tousled from the wind. He looked for ways to make her laugh, because her laugh had an infectious quality that roused a good feeling within him. He had it bad, he decided.

Go to bed. In the morning, rested, he'd be less— what? Smitten? Infatuated? Obsessed? He plopped on the bed. Enchanted.

Hazy sunlight streamed through lace curtains. In preparation for the heat, Tessa finished dressing in a lightweight sleeveless dress in pale green, then left the room and started down the stairs.

The rich aroma of coffee met her when her foot hit the last step. In the kitchen, he stood at the counter, pouring coffee from a black coffee brewer. He drew fantasies to a woman's brain. She watched big hands, callused and strong, and thought about them on her. How would they feel? What would his caress be like? She'd felt the touch of Harriet's lover. He'd been impatient, but gentle. Would Colby be tender or…

"Must be a doozy of a daydream."

Tessa snapped her attention to him. She'd kill herself if she blushed. *He can't read minds,* she reminded herself. "Good morning."

"Morning." His eyes stayed on her lips for a long moment, as if he planned another kiss. Or was she imagining the look? She needed to stop making so much of every glance her way.

"Do you want coffee?"

"Yes. Thank you." The faint, spicy scents of oregano and garlic lingered in the air. A clue that he cooked.

She took a seat at the round oak table and fingered a piece of a jigsaw puzzle that was half-finished and strewn across the table. She studied one piece that was shaped like a Y, then stared hard at the partially completed picture. "This is such a great kitchen." She meant that. It had a warm, homey feel. When she'd been a child, she used to imagine what the other kids' homes looked like. She'd have ranked this in the category perfect. "What is this a puzzle of?"

"A sailboat on the ocean."

She rolled her eyes. There was an abundance of tiny blue pieces. "Don't pick anything easy."

He gave her a wry grin. "I can scramble eggs, but if you want something else—"

She breathed deeply. "Coffee is enough."

He scowled at her. "No, it isn't. You can't go until lunch on only coffee."

"I'll buy a candy bar somewhere."

"Candy bars, lemon meringue pie. Junk food. You need to eat something that will get your feet moving."

She laughed. "Me or you? Are you trying to persuade me to make breakfast for you?"

"Me?" asked Mr. Innocence.

Tessa smiled and moved to the counter. "What would you like?"

As his hands went to her shoulders, a faint shock wave shot down her spine. "Sit down." He turned her around to head to the table. "I must have something that'll tempt you."

She searched for some simple way to tell him that she'd decided to go home. She needed to before she began to want too much. Her imagination could easily conjure up a more lasting visit. Perhaps that's what had been happening. Perhaps she hadn't felt anything really unusual at the first meeting. He was virile, sensual in a macho, tough way. Her imagination may have gone haywire over a really great-looking guy.

"No toast or cereal. Right?"

"Colby—"

He opened a cupboard door. "Aha."

"Aha, what?"

Like a prize, he raised one arm and dangled a bag of chocolate-chip cookies. "I knew I had something you'd like."

Tessa took his tease good-naturedly. The cookies were favorites of hers, the ones advertised as loaded with chocolate chips. "I'm really very easy to please—if you have leftover popcorn."

He set the bag on the table before her. "For breakfast? You eat that?"

With the sound of a cupboard closing, she craned her neck to see what he planned to eat as he brought out a box of cereal from the cupboard. A laugh rippled out. "That's a kid's cereal, Colby. Cocoa Munch 'n Crunch."

"Want some?"

"You phony."

"You, too." He held her with a look.

The seriousness came so quickly it threw her off balance. "What does that mean?"

"The store was always a cover-up, a way to get people to accept you."

She released a short laugh. "Hardly. You know that there are some people, like Leone, who believe I'm too odd for this town, believe I'm wacky, a space cadet because of what I sell."

"But that's easier, isn't it? The mumbo jumbo lets you hide."

"I'm hiding nothing. People know I'm psychic."

"They know now because of this investigation, but

except for a handful, most people don't believe it. And you want them to go on thinking that way. That's why you have the store. They can excuse something as a lucky guess by the eccentric who owns that store with the crystal balls.''

Tessa held firm beneath his scrutinizing stare. ''People accept eccentrics like fortune-tellers, but weird they have trouble with. I make a good living at fairs.''

''You said you don't predict.''

What was he trying to prove? He wouldn't understand. People never understood the foreboding that consumed her when she knew something wouldn't go well or the gray fog that took shape before her reeled images at her. ''I'll tell what is true now, but I don't predict anything that might alter the way a person lives.''

''Even if it's to protect them?''

Tessa looked away. He understood her better than she expected.

''You'll take risks to protect someone, won't you?''

More than once, she'd exposed herself to do just that. She'd been ridiculed. Worse. She'd been arrested. ''Yes, I will. How did you know?''

''My mother's feelings, not me, are what swayed you to help.''

Despite everything he'd said, she believed he was a man who'd never believe in her without irrefutable proof. He might be accepting her claim that she could see, but that didn't mean he believed.

"Who hurt you, Tessa?" he asked when she looked up.

He shouldn't have possessed such sensitivity. Louise had raised him well. But then he understood heartache, had experienced it, lost a love. Tessa pulled back, not letting herself connect with the hurt that he harbored. "We've all been hurt or disappointed at some time. It's part of living. Isn't it?"

He shrugged instead of answering and turned away to begin breakfast. A trace of melancholy shadowed Tessa. She'd always wished for a confidant, someone close, a best friend. *Will you be my best friend, Colby?* What man would want to live every day with someone others viewed as a freak? She'd seen the derision her mother had endured. If Tessa had learned any lesson, it was not to let people see too much of the real Tessa Madison.

"Before I can leave, I need to do a few chores," he said.

"I'll finish getting ready." She wasn't surprised that he'd asked no more. She thought he was dodging the truth in her question. They'd both been hurt. As she wanted to avoid the memory of her heartache, he was dodging his own. It was best for them not to share. There was too much intimacy in such an act, too much chance that she'd begin to believe in them.

After breakfast, she hurried to pack her things and make the bed. Minutes later, she entered the kitchen and looked out a window to see Colby crossing from the corral to the stables. He whipped off his Stetson and rubbed a forearm across his brow. Sunlight gleamed on his hair, casting blond highlights through the brown strands.

She pushed open the screen door and stepped outside. Leaning against a porch upright, she watched his long, easy stride while he entered the stable.

Slowly she descended the stairs. This was his home, the land that he loved. She'd seen a few ranches outside Rumor with weathered-looking buildings. At the bottom step, she rocked back on her heels and stared at the house, a white, two-story farmhouse with Wedgwood blue shutters. All the buildings were crisp and newly painted, displayed pride of ownership.

Pivoting, she took in the huge trees bordering the driveway. Sounds surrounded her. A horse snorted. In nearby trees, birds chirped. Men perched on the rails of the corral and yelled encouraging words to a cowboy who danced around a spirited colt while he tried to slide a bridle and reins over its head.

Beneath a bright sun promising another sweltering hot day, Tessa walked past the corral and entered the stable. Morning light spilled across several stalls. Horses whinnied as if in duet with the whirl of the fans. In each stall, one was positioned toward the horse to cool it off. As she stepped in, hay moved beneath the soles of her shoes. She was midway when she spotted Colby standing in one of the horse stalls beside a tan horse with a gorgeous white mane and tail. The pregnant one, Tessa knew. ''She's beautiful.''

He swung around, smiling. "I thought so."

"What's her name?"

He grinned. "Do you know?"

"Beautiful."

"That's not it.

"You're beautiful," Tessa cooed to the horse, running fingertips down her nose.

"She's the palomino that's supposed to be pregnant," he said as an introduction. "Ladyfair."

Tessa ignored the trace of skepticism in his voice. Soon enough he'd learn that she was right about the horse. "I know." She rested her face against the mare's. "No wonder you care so much for her. Who's her lover?" He chuckled, drawing her gaze to him. "That's funny?"

"Different. I've never heard anyone say that before. You're a romantic, aren't you, Tessa Madison?"

She knew that was true. She wanted to believe in happily ever after. She'd always hoped that Mr. Right really existed for her but had begun to doubt the possibility. "You didn't answer my question."

"A neighbor has a fellow for her. They've been together twice now." Though he shrugged as if not concerned, Tessa took a moment to concentrate and opened herself to his feelings, then knew differently. He loved this horse. He wanted her lineage to go on. Turning, she watched him move to a horse across the aisle. "You're really busy. I can't ask you to take time to help me."

"I'm almost done," he said, not looking back while he finished wiping down the horse to cool it.

"You wouldn't be here now if I hadn't gotten you involved." She returned his smile as he turned and faced her while he wiped his hands on a towel. "We need to find out who's so afraid of you. I doubt we'll get any answers about who bought those flowers, but we might try florists in Billings."

"I can't this morning." Tessa checked her wristwatch. "I have a shipment coming in. I can't have Marla lifting anything. She's pregnant."

He pulled a face. "I didn't know that."

Tessa stroked the mare's nose. "No one does."

"Does she?"

Tessa swung around. He looked stunned by his own question. Before he saw her smile, she turned away. Perhaps in his own way, he was beginning to believe in her.

Colby left Tessa in front of her store. He'd had a lousy night. But he'd told her no strings when he'd asked her to come to the ranch, and he was an honorable man. He was also a stupid one, he decided. Only a stupid man would make such a noble gesture.

He drove in the direction of the Kincaid ranch for a meeting with a neighbor whose son had started rodeo a few months ago. Colby had the perfect quarter horse for him.

He spent more time than he expected with father and son, answering questions not only about the horse but also about life on the rodeo circuit. Colby hadn't painted a pretty picture. Life was hard traveling from one rodeo to the next. Sometimes money was nonexistent. But he knew the boy already had rodeo fever and was deaf to Colby's words about the rough times.

By mid-afternoon, he was parking in front of Tessa's again. He couldn't believe he'd bought in to the clairvoyance bit, that he'd credited her with knowing some woman was pregnant before the woman did. Dumb. That was impossible. Her assistant had thrown up. Or something. With a shake of his head, he climbed out of the truck.

Grinning, Rumor's mayor stood on the sidewalk, waiting for him. Pierce Dalton's disposition had definitely improved since Chelsea Kearns came into his life. "I'm glad I ran into you, Colby. A shipment of fans is coming in day after tomorrow—"

Pierce didn't have to finish. "I'll be around to help deliver them," Colby cut in.

The mayor slapped his shoulder before turning away. "I wish everyone was so dependable."

Colby didn't envy him. He climbed the steps to the entrance door. The last thing he'd want to be was a politician, trying to appease everyone.

Smiling, Colby doffed his hat to two women coming out. As they passed, they whispered. He'd guess that rumors had begun to circulate about him and Tessa.

When he stepped in, Marla smiled so wide her face should have cracked. "Hi, Colby." Not for the first time, her voice sang when she talked to him. "If you're looking for Tessa, she isn't here now. She doesn't work today."

Why had she said she had to go to the store? "She said she was coming in."

"She did. And then she left."

Damn. So to be alone, she hadn't told him that she wasn't staying there. She could be in danger, didn't she realize that? "Where is she? Do you know?"

Marla shook her head. "I don't think she's home," she said, directing a look upward as if she could see through the ceiling into Tessa's home.

So where the hell was she? He left, cussing, wishing he knew where to look. But she wasn't easy to second-guess.

"Was that dang Pierce looking for me?" Henry called from a few feet away as Colby's boot hit the last step. "From down the block, I saw you talking to him."

Colby was in no mood for passing pleasantries with Henry. "I don't know if he was." He looked down the street. Where should he look for her?

Henry gestured with a thumb at Mystic Treasures. "You looking for *her?*"

He'd said the *her* with a disdain that made Colby narrow his eyes at him.

"She's at Whitehorn Memorial."

Colby swung around. "What?" Tension knotted his stomach. Had she been hurt? How badly? "What happened to her?"

"Oh, hell. There's Dalton." Henry started backing away.

"Dammit, Henry. What's wrong with her?"

"You should know best of all," he said with a

snideness that Colby let pass because he was too worried to bother with him. "You spend more time with her than anyone else."

"Is she hurt?"

"No, no." He kept backing up. "I don't have time to help Pierce. Tell him."

"You tell him," Colby yelled, hopping in his truck. He floored the pedal and hit the highway at a speed destined to get him a ticket. Henry said she wasn't hurt. Whatever she was doing at the hospital had nothing to do with her needing medical assistance, he reminded himself.

Chapter Eight

The drive to Whitehorn took forever, though Rumor was only twenty miles away. Halfway there, he recalled his mother's words about Tessa volunteering at the hospital and felt himself breathe normally for the first time since talking to Henry.

Still, after hurrying into the hospital, he checked at the emergency room desk. No Tessa Madison was there. Hunting her down seemed dumb. He could hardly go from room to room. He went down a corridor to find the nursing supervisor's office.

"Cowboy, are you lost?"

The gray-haired nurse looked sympathetic. Colby gave his head a brief shake as he realized he was on the maternity floor. "I'm looking for a friend. She's supposed to be here, but not in emergency. Tessa Madison."

"Tessa." The woman's face brightened. "I know Tessa. She's a volunteer here."

"Where would I find her?"

"She helps out with the children. Go to the children's floor."

Nothing was simple with her. Constantly she surprised him. As the elevator doors swooshed open, he stepped out, then wandered toward a crowd gathered at the end of the hallway. Several nurses lingered outside the doorway of a huge room. In the center of it was a clown in baggy orange-colored pants, an oversize green-checkered coat, too-big, bright yellow shoes that flopped when he walked, and a pink derby with a bright yellow daisy sticking up like an antenna. Carrot-red hair framed the face painted with white makeup. He blew up a bright pink balloon and twisted it into the shape of a bunny, then placed it in the hands of a young boy in a wheelchair, his right leg in a cast to the thigh.

The clown did a slow knee bend, then raised one white gloved hand and squeezed his giant red nose. It beeped, drawing a roomful of childish giggles.

Colby had caught the end of the clown's act. With a wave, the clown took two steps toward the door, backed up three, waved again, then scurried toward one little girl and gave her a squeezing hug before scampering toward the door. No more than five years old, the girl had sparse blond hair growing back to resemble a short cap. The girl beamed and waved goodbye.

Colby stepped to the side to let the clown pass, and

scanned the room filled with not only children but nursing staff, a few office employees and several other adults, volunteers, he assumed.

"Want a daisy?" a voice said from behind him.

He smiled even before he turned.

Holding out a gigantic yellow daisy, the clown smiled. "Or do you want a kiss, mister?" Lips outlined with bright red makeup puckered up. Beautiful gray eyes circled by black makeup danced with a smile.

He couldn't help grinning. "Could I collect one later?" He put a fingertip to the white makeup covering Tessa's face. "You have many talents." And few people knew about this. Special. Caring. "How long have you been doing this?"

"Since I came to town."

"Nice."

"It's nothing. I learned how to make the balloons while I was working in Chicago."

He grinned, thinking she looked adorable. "And the getup?"

"At a country fair, a clown came into my tent to have his fortune told. I did it for free so he'd show me how to put on the makeup." Her eyes shifted to the little girl she'd hugged. Laughing, she showed her balloon to one of the nurses.

"Is she okay?" Colby asked.

A softness entered her gaze. "Yes, she'll be fine now."

"Will she?"

"Yes. She's had a hard time of it for someone so

young, but she's a fighter. Her courage is mind-boggling." Her smile spread from the overdrawn mouth to dance in her eyes. "Why are you here? Were you looking for me?"

"You weren't supposed to go off alone." He curled fingers beneath her elbow to keep her from moving away. "It's dangerous for you, Tessa."

"I can't put my life on hold because of someone with twisted thinking." She placed a hand on his cheek. "I need to change. Do you want to wait until I come back?"

"That's why I'm here." Did she really think he'd leave her alone?

"Thank you for being concerned. I know you want me to stay at the ranch, to accept a bodyguard all the time, but I can't do it your way."

How could he argue? She was courageous, he realized, but that wasn't because she stood up to someone's scare tactics. With a touch, could she tell if one of these children would die? She said she knew this little girl was going to be all right. But what about the children she touched who wouldn't be? Did she feel their pain and grieve silently for what would happen later on? He wanted to understand. He wanted to help. He wanted her to be able to share with someone—him. At that moment, he realized that he didn't understand her ability, but he wasn't as filled with doubts as he'd once been.

Tessa strolled to him. "That wasn't long, was it? I thought it would take longer to get rid of the makeup." She slid the carryall containing her costume onto her shoulder. "How did you know where I was?"

"Henry."

Walking with him to the exit, she frowned. "How did he know?"

"He's the one who told me you were here. What's the problem?"

Tessa preceded him outside. "Why would he keep tabs on me?"

"He knew you volunteered here." Colby slowed his stride. "Do you think—"

Tessa shook her head. "No, I guess not The mayor's office has a list of people in Rumor who volunteer. That's probably how he knew about me. He hangs around the office as if he's still mayor."

"You're not off the hook, you know," Colby said before she stepped away. "You weren't supposed to go wandering around. There's someone out there who's trying to scare you."

"And doing a good job of it."

He was surprised at her admittance. Until now, except for conceding to stay at the ranch, she'd played gutsy lady to the hilt.

Tessa gestured toward her van. "I'm parked over there."

Colby pointed in the opposite direction. "I'm over there. I'll meet you at the ranch." He watched her head for her truck. She was such a contradiction. He'd liked her from day one even though he should have been wary of someone like her. Until she'd opened the shop, she'd hardly been the settling down type.

She'd admitted she'd traveled a lot with her mother. He figured in time she'd get bored living in Rumor.

He'd expected her to be eccentric, but during the past days, he'd been with a woman who'd donned a clown outfit to entertain sick kids, who'd rushed to work because she didn't want her employee, newly pregnant, lifting the boxes that were delivered. This was a woman who'd munch on popcorn or lemon meringue pie for breakfast, who told fortunes at county fairs. She was an enigma. Sensible yet kooky. Stubborn yet adaptable. Tough yet delicate.

And instead of keeping his distance, he sought her out at every free moment. Being with her was paramount in his mind. Lately that's all that mattered.

Colby stopped at a red light. In front of him, Tessa suddenly jumped out of her van and dashed toward his truck. Why? Concerned, he glanced around, saw nothing. Before she reached him, he opened the door and slid out from behind the steering wheel. ''What's wrong?''

''Nothing.'' She touched his arm. ''I'm sorry. I didn't mean to alarm you. I have an idea for dinner.'' She pointed across the street. ''See that supermarket?''

Tension oozed from him. ''You want to buy something special?''

''Yes. Okay?'' She didn't wait for his answer. With a glance at the light, she whirled and sprinted to her van before the light changed.

Smiling, Colby climbed into his truck. The unexpected. That's what she brought into his life.

* * *

Tessa couldn't believe that Mr. Steak and Potatoes had agreed to her suggestion to pick up Asian food from a cooked-to-order section.

While Colby opened a bottle of wine, she spooned portions of almond chicken and Mongolian beef from the white cartons. He sampled everything, then ate with gusto. Sipping her wine, she watched him over the rim of her glass. What would he say if she told him that a yearning taunted her whenever he stared at her?

"This is good," he said with a look at her.

"You ate all of it." She reached forward. "You'll love this," she said about the crab puff in her hand. He looked skeptical, but when she held it out to him, he took a bite. "Good?"

Chewing, he grinned and nodded his head. "Good," he mumbled.

"You're a good sport, Holmes."

He laughed. "So are you, Madison."

While he cleaned up the kitchen, Tessa called Marla. A regular was at the store, and two women from Billings bought merchandise. A good sign, Tessa mused, wandering to the kitchen. That meant people were learning about Mystic Treasures. "Can I help?"

"Done," he said, turning from the sink and facing her.

Tessa's heart quickened when he moved toward her. She laughed to relax herself as his arm snaked around her waist. Nothing felt steady. Her pulse raced at an uneven pace. Her heart pounded harder. She'd have hoped for promises but knew better. He wouldn't make them, and she'd learned never to expect them. "What do you want?" she asked even though she knew the answer.

His eyes met hers with a soft, understanding look that was more unsettling than one filled with desire. "No. What do you want?"

You weaken me. With his breath, warm and sweet, fanning her face, she only had to close her eyes to summon up his taste. Was this what desire was really supposed to feel like? She'd never wanted to be with someone like this, not even with Seth. So at twenty-four, Tessa Madison, resident psychic, was still a virgin. "I want to be with you," she said without hesitation. She'd known this was where they'd be one day. She'd felt the certainty of this moment on the first day she'd met him.

Softly he kissed her brow, her cheek, a corner of her lips, then looked down, drew her fingers to his lips, kissed them. Was she still breathing? she wondered.

With the pressure of his hand at the small of her back, almost testingly he brushed his lips across hers. She'd been dying for the feel of his arms around her again. "This is—" She paused as he directed his lips to the sensitive flesh at the curve of her neck.

"Whatever we want it to be," he murmured.

Tessa drew a long breath to relax the excitement pounding through her. They wouldn't let emotion get in the way. They'd go their separate ways eventually. But for now—for this night she wanted to be with him. She wanted whatever moments she could have with him.

Don't rush. Savor. Colby tried to bide his time, but he'd been fantasizing almost since their first meeting, wondering if she'd taste as sweet as she looked, imagining the velvety feel of pale skin beneath his caress. No hurry, he told himself, hoped he'd remember that once the excitement began and his body was bathed in the heat. As he wound fingers into her hair, he captured her mouth with his. He wanted to grind his mouth on hers, make his mark. He wanted her need to match his, wanted to feel desperation in her mouth answering his. He heard her soft whimper and lingered, but he felt no patience.

She fueled him, yanking his shirt from his jeans. Control was slim as her fingers moved over the buttons of his shirt. The touch was tentative, inexperienced, all the sweeter because of that. With his mouth on hers, he shrugged out of his shirt, felt a rush of need when her hands touched his skin, when slowly her fingertips traced a scar along his rib cage.

"A battle wound?" she murmured against his lips.

"From a bull's horn." He drew a deep breath, filling himself with her scent. Reaching behind her, he tugged at the dress zipper. Lightly he slid off first one shoulder and then the other. Cloth whispered beneath his hands and slithered over her hips to pool at her feet. He couldn't recall her stepping out of the dress. He couldn't think about anything but the lips twisting over his, the soft body straining against his.

In the feminine fingers pressing against his bare back, he felt tension. When he heard her sigh, he gathered her closer and lifted her into his arms.

Her eyes, hooded, held on his in the darkness of the staircase as he carried her to the bedroom. In the moonlit room, they sank to the bed. He fought with the lace and silk piece of material covering her breasts, inhaled her scent, the lavender fragrance, as if it were his air. He couldn't remember this neediness before.

On an oath, he pulled away to yank off boots. Those eyes that had haunted him from day one never left his while he stripped off his jeans. He came to her naked, touched the sharp point of her hip, the curve of her breast. Whatever he expected paled in comparison to the need driving him. Hungry for the touch of her skin, he took first one nipple and then the other in his mouth.

He'd planned to go slow, but then she touched him. Delicate fingers closed over him and nearly sent his head swimming. He hadn't expected her touch, hadn't been ready for it. Barely he held onto a slim grip of reality. A stroke from her, and he nearly lost it.

Turning on his side, facing her, he slipped his fingers between her legs to probe the moist softness of her. On a moan, she jolted beneath him. Give. That was his only thought. He waited a moment, then inched lower to spread kisses down her breast to her stomach. Desire clawed at him, but he wanted to give her more. From the first time he'd seen her, he'd wanted to be with her like this. When his breath heated the inside of her thigh, he heard her quick intake of air. Her scent and taste were a part of him now. As she arched, he stayed with her hot flesh a moment longer.

Then, heart pounding, he reached into the bedside table for the condom. Madness made him want to rush and bury himself in her softness.

For the first time in his life, he nearly fumbled opening the package.

She had to be ready. He was dying. It was his only thought before he crushed her mouth with a hard kiss and shifted to lie between her legs. She'd seduced him with her sweet taste, with her tentative touch. He remembered it and entered her gently. He'd planned to wait, offered only the tip. But she gripped his shoulders, and her legs embraced him. He couldn't wait. He entered her fully, felt the resistance, heard her moan. Silently he swore. And stilled. He was her first. "Tessa," he said between harsh breaths.

"Don't talk."

Talk. He could barely breathe. He wanted her to know he treasured this gift, but the frenzy had begun. Flesh rubbed flesh. Breaths became gasps. Through a cloud of sensation, he heard her uneven breathing. With one stroke after another, all that he was belonged to her. He rocked from the craving, plunged deeper, drove her with him.

Her soft groan blended with his. There was no waiting. Her warmth and softness enveloped him, and he moved with her, against her. *Pleasure her.* It was his only thought. When she cried out, when he knew

she'd peaked, he gave in to his own need. On a muf-
fled moan, he buried his face in the curve of her neck.
Tangled together, they rode the pleasure as one.

It had been wonderful. For a long moment, no other
thought would form in Tessa's mind. She'd never
cared to be with a man. She'd wanted the first time
to be special. But it had been wonderful because it
was him. She'd known, hadn't she? She'd known
she'd fall in love with him since that sultry Saturday
evening when she stood in the moonlight near a car-
nation-draped trellis with Sylvia and Larry's love in
the air. Yet she tried desperately to remember to expect nothing more than this.

Despite the mantle of darkness surrounding them,
when he braced himself over her, she could see his
face. "Tessa, why?" Against her breast, she felt the
hard beat of his heart, slowing. "Why didn't you tell
me?"

She laughed, but what she really wanted was for
him to touch her again, to press down on her again.
"It's not something you announce."

"I should have known." He looked disturbed, as
if he was battling to sound coherent when his face
was still bathed in the dampness of their lovemaking.
"You were vulnerable. That wasn't right."

"I chose you," she said simply, because that was
the truth.

"You chose me?" Staring at her, he gave her a
half grin. "Are you kidding?"

He might feel tricked, she realized. She'd invited,

responded, answered his kiss. Couldn't he tell how much she'd wanted him? He must know he excited her in a way she'd never known before. She'd thrilled when his body was against her, in her. She'd felt weak with dizzying pleasure yet strong with the power he gave her when they'd made love. "You chose me, too," she said, hoping he'd settle for that explanation. "It was wonderful. You were wonderful." On a sigh, she slid a hand around the back of his neck to let her fingers wander into his hair. She loved the way she felt in his arms. She loved the taste of him.

"That was my line," Colby whispered close to her ear.

Tipping her head back, she opened her mouth invitingly to him. This felt so right, so good.

A similar thought came to mind when she stood in his kitchen the next morning. Distractedly she measured coffee grounds into the brewer basket while she recalled last night.

She felt so alive, different—loved. She didn't think this was the way every woman felt after her first time. Only someone in love. She felt as if they were a part of each other now. She knew there was danger in making too much of last night. But she had no regrets. For her, it had been a memory she'd hold close to her heart forever.

Only anticipation shadowed her as she wondered if they'd have another night together. He'd acted as if he wanted her. He'd said she was wonderful.

She'd surprised herself, but she'd liked touching him. She liked what she made him feel. She loved what he did to her. *Slow down,* she warned herself. So many times she'd seen the heartbreak her mother had gone through because she believed in love. Tessa couldn't afford to expect too much. She'd have no expectations, look for no promises. With eyes wide open, she'd spend time with him and love him for a while.

"I was looking for you."

She hadn't heard his approach. A gentle hand on her belly swayed her back into him as if they were meant to be as one. She drew a deep breath, inhaled his scent. "Did you have a reason?" She barely managed to speak with his lips caressing the sensitive skin below her ear.

"The best," he murmured.

She'd always hoped for someone special, someone who wouldn't be afraid to be with her. But the more content she was with him, the more she wanted to have. And she felt suddenly afraid, aware how much she could be hurt from wanting too much. "Coffee's done." She slipped out of his embrace before he saw the frown stirred by her thoughts.

With her movement, he swung toward the table and reached for his cup. Over her shoulder, she saw him grimace at the package of coconut-covered marshmallow cupcakes she'd purchased from a vending machine in town yesterday.

"Get that, will you, Tessa?"

A second passed before she heard the doorbell. Obviously he wasn't concerned that Harriet's killer stood outside his front door or he wouldn't have asked her to answer it. Since he was busy at a cupboard, she rushed across the living room to the door. "I'm coming," she called and opened the door. Sick. Immediately she felt sick.

"Tessa Madison?"

She heard the delivery man, but couldn't stop staring at the long white florist's box.

"Here you are."

She couldn't find her voice. The box was in her arms. She watched the man turn away without receiving a tip. How could the person trying to scare her know she was here?

Chapter Nine

Tessa swung around with the box cradled in her arms and saw Colby standing in the kitchen doorway. "Look."

By the expression on his face, she knew she'd paled. In a few strides, he crossed to her, enveloped her in his arms. "Tessa. They're from me. I'm sorry. That was damn insensitive of me."

Still cradling the box, she shot a look at him. "You sent them?"

"God, you're white. I never thought you'd get scared when you saw them. It was a dumb idea."

"No, it wasn't," she quickly replied. She was becoming a weak little girl. When had she ever let herself become so unnerved so easily? "It was a great idea." She needed to overcome the sense of dread she had every time she saw flowers. In an excited rush to see what he'd sent, she whipped the red ribbon off the box, then lifted the lid. Her heart quickened. A dozen perfectly shaped red roses and wispy-looking ferns were nestled in the green tissue. "Oh, Colby." Her throat tightened. The tears came unexpectedly.

With his fingertips, he caught her chin. "I didn't buy them to make you cry. I thought you needed to get ones that would make you smile. Unfortunately they didn't affect you that way."

Tessa laughed in response to the good humor in his voice. "Oh, but they did. These are tears of joy. Thank you. It was so nice of you." She raised misty eyes to meet his. "Thank you for reminding me how wonderful it is to get them like this, how beautiful they are." She lifted the flowers to take in their fragrance. "Do you have a vase?"

"A vase?" He grinned wryly. "Now there's something I've had a lot of need for." Keeping her close, he walked her to the kitchen. "I have a glass pitcher." He turned to retrieve the pitcher from a cabinet. "A big one. My mother told me it was for iced tea."

From the way he said that, she doubted he'd ever made any. She joined him by the sink, watched water fill the pitcher. "The pitcher is fine, really," she said, not knowing what could be stirring his frown.

"Can you take the day off? We need to get some answers. We might find some in Billings."

"Check florists? Find out who sent the dead flowers?"

"It's an idea." He faced her. "You can't live in fear. I brought this on you. I have to do something to stop it."

Tessa didn't bother to argue. If she had, he'd have gone alone. He was hoping she might feel something at one of the florists if she went with him. She thought it might be a good idea. As much as she loved his attention, he couldn't play her bodyguard twenty-four hours a day.

When they drove through Whitehorn, Colby slowed the truck to practically a standstill for the posted speed-limit outside Whitehorn Memorial Hospital. Tessa viewed the jagged peaks of the Crazy Mountains to the west. She'd stopped in this town when she'd arrived in Montana and had driven to the Stop N Swap. She'd expected only the owner of the junk store, Winona Cobb, to be there, but her niece, Crystal Cobb, now Ravencrest, had been there, too. They'd connected immediately. Because of their psychic powers, they were kindred souls. Tessa had visited Winona several times on days when she did her volunteer work at the hospital.

It was afternoon when Colby drove them into Billings. In passing, Tessa noticed that a local park was empty. The heat smothered, discouraging summertime picnics or softball games. An American flag on a pole hung limply from lack of any breeze. At a lazy pace, Tessa strolled with Colby along the sidewalk and wandered into a florist shop.

By four o'clock, visits to several similar shops had

proven futile. "If the flowers weren't ordered from a florist here, I doubt the pen was bought at one of the stores," Colby said when they stepped outside again.

Tessa stared at the display window still showing floral arrangements with Fourth of July colors. "The proverbial search for the needle in the haystack," she said and fought drooping spirits. If they could discover the name of Harriet's lover, the person who gave her the pen, they might narrow down possibilities. At the least, they might be able to eliminate Harriet's lover as the killer. Tessa gestured toward a gas station with a quick-stop market. "Do you think they sell pens?"

He scanned the street of businesses, then opened the truck door and removed the last box of dead flowers she'd received. "Let's try that florist over there."

The woman inside the shop was a sweet grandmotherly-looking type with silver hair. "Roses are for lovers." Since they'd entered, she'd repeatedly looked from Tessa to Colby. "You really are a lovely couple. I suppose everyone tells you that."

"Everyone," Colby confirmed, slipping an arm around Tessa's waist. "We were told it was written in the stars."

The woman beamed. "Oh, how romantic." As she turned away to answer her phone, Tessa gently elbowed him in the ribs. "You're an incorrigible tease, aren't you?"

"Guilty." He grinned, still looking pleased when the woman returned to them. "We need help," he said, bringing the conversation to the business at hand. He opened the box to reveal the flowers.

"Oh." The woman clucked her tongue. "They're dead. I'd never send dead flowers. And I don't use that kind of box," she said, tapping a finger on it.

"Do you know who might?"

"Someone who buys inferior flowers for their arrangements."

Colby prodded. "Like?"

"Morton's Mortuary has a florist adjacent to their building. They're not too particular there."

"Where is it?" Colby questioned.

She gave them an address and whispered a departing suggestion to Colby. "Red roses. They'd be perfect for her."

The man at the mortuary, an Ichabod Crane look-alike who held his hands together in a gesture of prayer, informed them in his quiet, monotone voice that they acquired their flowers from a nursery in Boise. They made a quick check with the florist next door. It had no record of delivering any flowers in Rumor.

Tessa sighed. "One dead end after another."

"I'll check out Boise," Colby said.

She thought he might be wasting his time, but said nothing rather than go head-on with his stubborn streak. "Did you bring the pen?" Tessa asked, eyeing a greeting card shop across the street.

"I have it." He fished in his shirt pocket and removed the gold pen with its fine point.

Tessa viewed it as a gift for a practical woman. Had Harriet's lover understood she'd treasure that more than a bottle of perfume? Or had Harriet felt disappointment at not receiving something more romantic?

"Let's go over." Colby placed a hand at the small of her back to urge her toward the store. "We might have some luck."

They had none.

"The pens can be bought in any stationery or greeting card store," the woman manager in the nationwide chain store told them. "And engraving is usually offered."

"She made the pen as a gift seem like nothing special," Tessa said when they stepped outside. "It might have been a practical gift, but if it was from a man Harriet cared deeply about, it would be special to her. Don't you think so?" she asked when they were in the truck.

Colby switched on the ignition. His lips curved in a wry grin that carried a hint of sadness. "She'd value something that was useful."

As he turned on the CD player, she dropped her head onto the headrest and listened to the music, country songs, mostly about love. "We came up empty today."

Colby looked away from the traffic. "I know a way to keep the day from being a total waste."

She saw the flash of his smile and laughed. "I know you do. So do I. Let's go horseback riding."

She saw his look of surprise. "You thought I couldn't?"

"I thought you were a city girl."

"Fooled you."

Atop his horse, a deep brown with a patch of white on its chest, Colby took the lead. Slowly he rode Dancer down a trail that snaked around trees away from the ranch and toward a lake. He gave a sweep of his arm. "Best place in the world."

Tessa brought the roan alongside Dancer. "Oh, it's lovely here," she said as the lake came into view between the trees.

Colby thought she was. Sunlight gleamed on her hair, casting silver streaks through the raven color. With her nearness, he caught her light, flowery scent. Desire was only a breath away, he realized. "It's a great place to go fishing."

"Fishing?" A smile swept over her face. After hours that had held too much seriousness, she was grateful that he'd thought of a way to lighten their day.

He reined Dancer at a grassy spot where wildflowers sprinkled color on a nearby path. "Where did you learn to ride?"

"We lived in Texas for a while." As Colby dismounted, so did she. Perspiration trickled down her back. "My mother had a brief relationship with a rancher." So often her mother had gotten attached to some man and then watched him leave after one of her visions.

He tethered the reins on a nearby tree branch. "Pick a spot."

While she chose two boulders near the bank and beneath a tree, he grabbed the fishing poles and tackle box from behind his saddle. "Is this a favorite spot of yours?"

"Garrett and I used to skip school and come here. Until my dad caught us, I'd miss for days."

"And ace the tests?"

"Usually." Colby settled on the rock beside her. "Everything came easy," he admitted. A gentle breeze fluttered her hair. With a featherlight touch, he tucked a strand behind her ear.

"I always liked going."

He leaned over, kissed her gently, softly, tenderly. "Bet you were a cutie."

Tessa laughed. Pleasurable warmth moved through her. "Oh, stop." She cast a look around. "Any girl's initials carved on a tree in a heart?"

"Nope. Want yours?"

His question made her smile. When she'd been young, Tessa would have loved it if some boy had said that to her. How many girls had he made such an offer to? She wondered, aware he'd known his share while traveling the rodeo circuit. "Do you miss rodeo, Colby?"

His head bent, he stared into his tackle box. "That was a different life. It gave me thrills. But this is just as satisfying, in a different way. Let's see if you're really any good at this."

Shifting on the hard rock, she raised her face to a

bright sun. It promised to deliver another sweltering day. "I never back away from a challenge, Colby. I saw you, you know. Years ago."

"You mean—" He wiggled fingers in front of his eyes. "That kind of saw me?"

Tessa stifled a giggle. "Yes. I saw you in a rodeo in Texas. Ten years ago."

Despite the brim of his hat shading his face, she saw his grin. "Why would you remember me?"

"Because I was fourteen." She took the rod from him, then peered into the tackle box for a lure. "Because you were eighteen and—"

He looked away from the water, shimmering beneath late-afternoon sunlight. "And what?"

And I was a dreamy-eyed teenager. Stalling, she pretended intense interest in the lures. "Gorgeous," she answered while she chose a three-prong hook with a red-and-white stripe.

He sounded pleased. "You thought I was gorgeous?"

"Remember, I was fourteen. Easily impressed." Tessa laughed at his pseudo-withering look.

"Did you like the rodeo?"

"It was fun." She paused to cast her line. "I held my breath the whole time you were on the horse." She'd sat on the bleachers, captivated by the lean, cute cowboy. She'd listened to the buzzer, the cheers of the crowd and hadn't been able to take her eyes off him. "I plan to catch the first fish."

Colby hooked his line before slanting a look at her.

"Are you trying mental telepathy to catch one?"

"My magic power," she teased.

He leaned close and nuzzled her neck. "I know. It's potent."

She turned her face so her mouth met his, but at the last second jerked back, letting his lips kiss air. "Oh! I think I've got one."

"You just put your line in. You couldn't have—"

Definitely she felt the tug on the pole. "Tell the fish that," she said, reeling in the line. "Oh, Colby." The fish splashed the top of the water. "Oh, look. Look what I've got."

"Reel it in."

"I am, I am," she said excitedly. "It's big, isn't it?"

He started laughing. "I don't believe it."

"How big is it?"

"Big enough. You're amazing, Madam Tessa."

"Can you cook this?" she asked, not taking her eyes off the fish.

"I know someone who can."

Colby waited until they were in the truck driving toward town before he made the phone call. As he expected, his mother was agreeable. With a goodbye, he set his cell phone on the seat beside him. "My mother said bring the fish. She'll make the rest of the dinner."

"That's nice of her." Tessa sniffed hard. "I smell fishy."

He thought she smelled like wildflowers. "That's because you hugged the fish."

Tessa pulled a face at his tease. "The way it was flopping around, I thought I'd lose it. I won't be long, but I need to take a quick shower."

"Okay. I'll go see Holt while you do that." He braked in front of Mystic Treasures, thought about going in to check rooms but knew she'd resist. "I shouldn't be too long."

"I'll be waiting." Leaning close, she placed a hand on his shoulder, pressed her breasts into him and kissed him hard.

"Tessa," he said when she drew back.

On a laugh, she jumped out of the truck. "Later."

Effortlessly she knocked him off balance, he realized as he watched her dash up the stairs to the store. Sharp, conflicting emotions moved through him whenever he thought of her, was with her. She made him feel more than he had in a long time. In little ways, she managed to surprise him, made him laugh more than any woman ever had. It felt so damn good to feel good.

He was still smiling when he entered the police department a few minutes later.

"I was coming to see you," Holt said in greeting. Sitting at his desk, the deputy sheriff was munching on a powdered sugar doughnut.

"Got any news?" Colby asked.

Holt's expression remained grim. "You won't like it."

"Did you learn more?" Tessa asked as soon as they were settled in Colby's truck.

"Some." Driving, he kept his eyes on the dark road. "Holt's been checking into Parrish's past."

He'd been so quiet, too quiet. "You were hoping he could be linked to the murder."

"He was my number one suspect," Colby said with a glance away from the road.

Tessa shifted on the seat to see him better in the dark confines of the truck. "Was?" She ran a smoothing hand over her lap in the peach-colored dress with its scooped neck and short sleeves. "He isn't anymore?"

"I wish he was, but Holt told me that Parrish has an airtight alibi for the night of Harriet's murder."

"Are they positive?"

A trace of irritation edged his voice. "He has the best one he could have. He was in a Kansas City jail for disorderly conduct. My parents won't be pleased."

Louise met them at the front door of her home. At Colby's brighter than usual greeting, Tessa assumed he would stall before announcing what he'd learned.

"Come in the kitchen," Louise urged.

Tessa stood in the living room of the country house and viewed the beamed ceiling and redbrick fireplace. She followed Louise across the highly polished wood floor and through a dining room with its bay window and window seat. "You have a lovely home."

"Thank you. It's taken a lot of years of fixing it up."

The kitchen was enormous and sunny with a wallpaper design of little yellow teapots on the wall above the sink and a knotty pine floor.

"This is one fine fish you caught, Tessa." Colby's dad lifted the fish Colby had cleaned at his house. "My son loves trout."

"They both do," Louise said to Tessa.

Colby gave her a grin before opening the refrigerator.

"Do you plan on telling us what's wrong?" Bud asked.

Tessa was surprised by his father's words. She'd thought Colby had done an admirable job of hiding his annoyance about Warren Parrish.

He faced his parents while yanking the tab off the beer can. "I didn't want to ruin dinner."

"You won't. Tell us," his mother urged. As he shared the news, her frown deepened.

Under his breath, Bud muttered something indecipherable.

Clearly they had been hoping that Warren Parrish was a suspect and would be out of their lives soon.

In response to the distress on his mother's face, Colby offered encouragement. "It only means that Parrish isn't the killer, but it doesn't mean that he's won, Mom."

Sadness lingered in her eyes. "I couldn't stand that man the moment I met him. You never got a vision about him?" Louise asked.

Tessa wished she could have given them information. "No. If I don't feel something right away, it's unlikely I will later." She moved closer to Louise. "Let me help with dinner."

"We all will," Bud said.

Louise pointed at her son. "You bread the fish. Tessa, you can mix the coleslaw. I'll start frying."

Tessa grinned at Colby. "Now I know why you're a good cook."

He slipped an arm around her waist. "Learned at my mother's knee."

"Don't believe him," his father quipped. "He learned while traveling so he wouldn't starve."

"A lot of hot dogs and beans during the lean years," Colby responded.

Bud laid a hand on his son's shoulder. "There weren't many of those. You won your share of prize money."

"He worried me sick," Louise said.

"She was always afraid he'd break a leg," his father said.

Louise looked up from the frying pan. "I was more concerned he'd become taken with one of those groupies who chased after him."

"Most of them are teenagers, Lou," Bud reminded her.

"Some aren't." She slid the spatula under the potato slices frying in the pan, then glanced askance at Tessa. "They're the ones that really worried me."

"Mom," Colby said in an affectionate, scolding tone.

Tessa veiled a smile.

Merrily, Louise went on. "Lots of women were taken with who he was, not who he is."

"They were knocking down my door, Mom," Colby said on a laugh.

"You weren't ever lonely, were you?"

Tessa had heard that he was a favorite not only because of his skill and winning record but also because of his charm and good looks.

"You've heard about the wrong kind of women," Louise said with a look at Tessa. "The last two years when he was earning lots of money it got worse."

A handsome champion with money would be considered a prize catch, Tessa mused. But she was confused. During that time, he'd been engaged to Diana Lynscot. Was Louise talking about her?

"Could we discuss something else?" Colby asked, looking comically pained rather than annoyed.

Tessa laughed at their easy camaraderie but wasn't surprised by it. From the moment she'd met Louise, she'd liked her sense of humor. Bud Holmes was just as likable and easygoing as his wife.

Conversation shifted from Colby's ranch to the previous baseball game on television. When Colby told them about her dilemma, Louise touched her hand. "What a dreadful thing to have happen. You need to learn the name of the person sending those flowers. I can't believe the problems going on in Rumor right now."

"They'll all be taken care of soon," Colby's dad said to soothe her. "And we'll have a celebration dinner then. We'll expect you to be here," he said to Tessa.

"I'd like that," she answered. They were so warm and welcoming, she wished she would be. Tonight had been another first for her. They'd known about her and still had made her feel comfortable, welcomed. Most parents of the men she'd dated acted as if they should hang garlic on the door to keep her away. Maybe that's why a tinge of melancholy swept over her after saying goodbye. Though she hoped to maintain a friendship with Louise, she doubted she'd be with the three of them like this again.

Waiting outside for Colby, she sat on the porch swing. The warm night air carried no breeze, and she placed a hand to the dampness at the back of her neck. The heat was making some people cranky, for good reason. Every day that passed, the woods got drier and the chance of fire became greater.

Sitting back, she pressed her heel on the porch and swayed, let her mind drift to business. She needed to change the front display window from...

"Get out!"

She stood in a room with an easy chair, a reading lamp and table. "Get out!" she yelled at his back. "Is that why you really came here tonight? How can you ask that of me? It's yours." Fury filled her. "I won't get rid of the baby."

"I don't want it."

He sliced her open with those words. "It doesn't matter to me what you want."

"Get rid of it. Or else." He swung away, stormed toward the door.

Tessa jerked at the image. He'd turned. She saw the buttons on his shirt, but his face was blurred. That made no sense. Everything else was clear. She'd even seen the numbers on the face of Harriet's wristwatch.

"Tessa, can you hear me?"

The feminine voice, the gentle touch of a hand on her shoulder brought her to her surroundings, but for a long moment, she stared at Louise's face. "Did your sister sit here often?"

"Whenever she visited."

"What about the last time you saw her?"

"Yes. She was here on the morning of her death. She seemed distracted. Why do you ask? Did you have a vision, Tessa?"

"Yes, I did."

Anticipation came into Louise's dark eyes.

Tessa rushed her words. "But I didn't see the killer's face." To tell her that in her vision Harriet's lover wanted her to get rid of the baby would have served no purpose except to sadden Louise more.

Colby kissed his mother's cheek. "Go in, Mom."

She gave him a wan smile. "I'm sorry. I was hopeful."

Tessa stood and hugged her. "I'm the one who's sorry. I wish I could give you more." Tessa waited until Louise stepped inside. "I saw only his back, Colby."

He slipped an arm around her shoulder. "It's okay."

"No, you don't understand. He's faceless."

"I know, Tessa. You told me that before. You—" As she balked, he stilled. "That's not what you mean, is it?"

"He hides."

Even in the shadows of night, she saw his confusion, said no more. He didn't want to believe in her visions.

She remained quiet during the drive to the ranch, but when they stepped onto the porch, she had to tell him what she felt. Someone needed to know. "Colby, he hides from everyone," she said, placing a hand on his arm to stop him from unlocking the door.

"I don't understand. What do you mean? You can't see his face because he's hiding from you?"

"No, he hides from everyone. They—we—all of us see a different person. Like your aunt had seemed rigid, even straitlaced, hardly the type to be even dating a man, and—"

"Was actually having an affair. Is that what you mean?"

"Sort of. This person is two-faced. No one knows the real person."

"Then it is someone we know?"

"The lover is. Yes. I think the reason I can't see the man's face is because I know him. I feel so badly. I wish I could have helped more."

"It's all right."

How easily he said that. Was that because he'd never believed she'd be any help? She pushed away the wave of sadness sweeping over her. *Don't spoil the time with him, Tessa.* "I'm sorry that you didn't catch any fish today," she said when they stepped inside his home.

"That's not why I went fishing."

"*You* didn't want to catch any fish?" No man used to winning would like an unsuccessful day doing anything.

"I had more time with you. That's why I suggested going."

With a few words, he made her feel so wanted. She'd never look for promises, but she was yearning for them. "And what did you learn?"

"There's a lot I don't know about you."

A gentle hand touched her hip, drew her to him. "Is this going to be twenty questions time?" she teased.

"I know you like horses. That's all I need to know."

"Easy to please."

"I know we both like to play pool."

She sensed that he was striving to keep the mood light. She wanted that. She didn't want to explore their relationship too deeply. "That doesn't count."

"I know you can rig the line and take a fish off a hook."

Tessa relaxed against him. "Incredibly important."

"What's more important?" he murmured, pulling her to him.

"That you're responsible, sensible, practical, logical," she reminded him.

"And you're not?" His voice came out softer, caressing. "Is that the point you're trying to make? Tessa, you're responsible. You have a business. You get up every morning and open it to customers."

Despite his seriously said words, Tessa saw a game beginning. "And you think I'm sensible?" Most people viewed her shop as nonsensical. Therefore, as owner, she was, too.

"And rational."

He was serious, she realized. This wasn't lip service. He believed she was responsible and rational.

"You're clearheaded."

She felt like laughing. She was so accustomed to different comments. Absurd. Wacky. Spacey. "Why do you think that?" she asked, trying to understand what made him see her differently.

A smile darkened his eyes. "You have good survival instincts. When Leone came after you, you kept your head, didn't argue, didn't agitate her."

He had no idea how much his compliments were touching her. "What about practical?" No one who owned a store offering unicorns and good-luck charms and objects to see into the future could be considered practical.

"That might be a stretch." He looked down as she began to unbutton his shirt. "I think you have a romantic streak, like to believe in fantasy."

She placed her palms against his bare chest. "So I'm not practical?" she challenged lightly.

"Doesn't matter. You have other fine qualities." Absently he toyed with a strand of hair near her cheek. "You're clever. Imaginative."

Beneath the gentle caress of his fingers along her spine, her eyes nearly closed. "That isn't the same."

His breath blended with hers. "Quit examining this, Tessa." Lazily he kissed her jaw. "Just go with it. Why are you so afraid of us?"

The question forced her to remember what she'd tried not to think about. She'd always believed that no man would ever accept such an oddity as hers in the woman he loved. She'd believed that her so-called gift had cursed her to a life without love.

"I asked you once before who hurt you. Tell me," he said against her cheek. "Trust me, Tessa."

She gave her head a shake. "It happened years ago."

"That doesn't make it any less important to you."

"Few people understand or accept my clairvoyance."

He inclined his head, forcing her to meet his stare. "Someone you cared about didn't?"

Tessa stepped free of his embrace. "Yes," she admitted. "His name was Seth. Years ago, I was with friends on a trip at a resort when I had a vision. I saw one of them falling, screaming. I told him about the vision. He laughed. So did Seth." He'd made fun of her. "He said that I thought I had Gypsy blood and could tell fortunes." She remembered how humiliated she'd been by his words, his ridicule.

Colby closed the inches she'd placed between them. "And you loved him?"

She made herself look up, knew he wouldn't let her stop now. "I was young." She met his serious dark stare. "I thought I loved him, so it hurt later, when we were alone, when he yelled at me. He was furious, claiming I'd made a fool of him, that because of me, his friends were laughing behind his back for having me as a girlfriend."

"What did you do then?"

"I couldn't go anywhere until the next day because of where we were. The next day, the friend who was an experienced backpacker was climbing a mountain with friends, and he fell."

"He—"

She watched his eyes, disbelief, the longing to comprehend, to make sense of something.

"What did he say?"

"When Seth heard about his friend's injury, he stared at me as if—" She took a deep breath. The old hurt rose so swiftly she was unprepared for it. She swallowed hard against the knot in her throat. "He stared at me as if I was weird, abnormal. He said that he never wanted me to do that—whatever the hell that was—again. I left him within the hour. I couldn't change for him, for anyone."

"He was a jerk."

"He was afraid," Tessa countered. "Aren't you?"

As if it were the most natural thing in the world, Colby opened his arms to her. "Only of how much you make me feel."

Tessa nearly stopped breathing. "I can't change." She felt compelled to remind him.

In the dim light of the room, his eyes looked darker. "I'm not asking you to change."

Chapter Ten

For so many years, Tessa had been alone. With those words he'd said to her, she'd wanted to cry. He knew more now, and he hadn't turned away.

After another night together, she was beginning to wish for everything she'd never believed was possible. She knew how foolish that was. Her mother had had the same hopes often. And each time a new man had come into her life, he'd left her bitterly disappointed. Tessa had watched her pain, had vowed after Seth never to leave herself unprotected. She had failed. She'd be hurt. There was no way to prepare for the end with Colby.

Standing by the kitchen sink, Tessa turned on the spigot to wash up the few glasses in it. For a moment, she watched water rush into the sink, then added dishwashing liquid.

On the windowsill before her was a miniature wood carving of a horse. Was it a childhood memento? Colby must carry fond feelings for the person who'd given it to him. She reached forward to pick it up. Had Louise or Colby's father or maybe Diana…?

No fog drifted over her. A vision slammed at her. *Her head jerked to the left. Her cheek burned from a slap. She ached elsewhere, too. Her hip. Oh, it hurt badly. She pressed her back to the wall, wanted to rub the sore hip. No time. She needed to get out. Run. Almost to the door, almost away.*

Her head exploded. She touched the back of it. It hurt, throbbed. She couldn't stand, couldn't keep her balance. Her legs felt funny, weak. Sinking. She was sinking to the floor now. If only she could rest. Just for a moment.

"Leave me alone." Why was she being hauled to her feet? Can't stand. "Please, leave me alone." Another shove. Into the chair. She tasted something wet, salty. She ran the tip of her tongue over the corner of her lip. There was blood. Her blood.

Fear filled her. He was so angry. How could someone be so angry? With a fingertip, she touched her lip and winced. Blood was on her finger. Wait. Be sure he isn't looking. Quickly she printed H, then I on the book. She snuck a glance his way, managed one more letter.

A pillow. Why did he have the pillow? Oh, my God. My gun. "Don't. Don't. Please. Don't kill my baby. My baby."

Tessa straightened with a start, shuddered with

Harriet's fear. Devastating fear. Not for herself, but
for her unborn child. Her baby. All Harriet had been
thinking about at the last moment had been the life
within her.

Looking down, Tessa retrieved the wood carving
from the sudsy water. Her throat felt raw. The pillow
had been used to muffle the sound of the gun. Who
had killed Harriet? Had the man been her lover? Tessa
knew because of a previous vision that Harriet had
fought with him about having the baby. But who had
killed Harriet? Why weren't the visions clearer?

She dried the wooden horse, then wandered toward
the screen door. As she stepped onto the porch, scents
of livestock, leather and ragweed mingled in the air.
Something was different this time. She should have
seen more. Why couldn't she?

She concentrated on Colby strolling toward her to
calm herself. A miscalculation on her part, she realized. Just looking at him made emotion swell within
her.

"Ready to head into town?" he asked from feet
away.

"Yes." She thought about the vision. She'd been
with Harriet at the moment of her death. He didn't
need to know that, and she wasn't ready to discuss
anything else about the vision.

"Why so quiet?"

She gave him a smile. "I was wondering about
Harriet. What she was like." She'd been getting
mixed signals about the woman. She'd heard that

Harriet was distant, even cool, but she'd proven she was caring by helping others.

"She wasn't easy to get close to. And she grew more distant during the last few months."

"Were you close at one time?"

Colby strolled with her to the truck. "Closer when I was a kid."

Tessa knew now what she'd felt by his kitchen sink. "There's a wood carving of a horse on your windowsill," she said once they were on the road. "Was that from…"

"It was from my aunt. She knew how much I loved horses. She gave that to me before I competed and won a prize in my first junior rodeo."

She knew why touching the wood carving of the horse had triggered a vision. "And you kept it?"

"I considered it a good-luck piece. It was always with me when I was on the rodeo circuit."

Tessa touched his arm. "That must have pleased her to know that it brought you good luck."

"I guess so." Because he was quiet for a long moment, she wished he hadn't slid on sunglasses, wished she could see his eyes. "The only time I ever saw her close to tears was the first time she walked into my kitchen and saw that I'd placed that wood carving on the windowsill. I didn't have much furniture then, but her gift was there."

Clearly Harriet had meant a great deal to him. Without planning to, Tessa slid beneath the surface of his pain, felt the heaviness of his grief. *I'm getting too close,* she realized in that moment.

Deliberately she thought about the store, about inventory, about requests from customers, anything to block the energy stretching from him to her. But her mind returned to unanswered questions about Harriet, to Colby's anguish for the loss of someone dear, to that vision of a woman pleading for the life of her unborn child.

Every morning Colby saw that wood carving, but until Tessa had mentioned it, he hadn't thought about when he'd received it. Since his aunt's death, he hadn't let memories of her come. For all her outward gruffness, his aunt had shown him her soft heart often. He'd been touched by her affection and compassion. When he'd been a kid, before she'd left for Boston, he'd lost his cat, Rennie. He'd fought tears. If his mom had been around, he'd have let the sadness out, but she'd been in Boise, taking care of Colby's grandmother. His father had gone through the rituals, helped him bury the calico. His aunt had gone one step further.

She'd met him after school the next day. She'd brought the flowers and the small wood cross with the name Rennie on it. They'd put the cross and the flowers on the grave, and then she'd wrapped her arms around him and had let him cry.

She'd been the one who'd forced him to grieve. Ironically, he couldn't do it now for her. Instead pain bottled within him. Like a pressure cooker, he sometimes felt as if he'd explode from it. Then he'd move away from thoughts of her, and the feeling would ease again—until the next time he'd remember how special she'd been to him. If wishes worked, he'd wish for a couple of seconds that he could be six again.

Colby dropped her off at the store, and Tessa spent the morning unpacking crates of new merchandise. She'd taken a financial chance, ordering more items, but she thought business would pick up by the end of the month after a psychic fair in another town.

Her back aching from bending over the crates, she straightened and stretched. She thought about the vision she'd had at Colby's house. Poor Harriet. How short-lived her happiness had been. At the end of her life, she'd become so sad. At the end, she'd been so frightened.

"Tessa, Tessa," Marla said in a loud whisper. "We have a customer."

Puzzled by her need to make such an announcement, Tessa wandered to the storeroom doorway and found herself face-to-face with Diana Lynscot. The next few moments might not be pleasant, she decided. "Hi," she said with her brightest smile. "Is there something in particular you're looking for?"

Diana's eyes moved over her. "No. I came in to see what you have that is attracting people to your store."

People meaning Colby.

"I suppose there are those who might be amused by the notion of the unusual and of love potions and trinkets."

Tessa wasn't letting her devalue the store. "We

have customers who take a more serious approach to what's offered here.''

Standing by the counter, Marla slapped a hand over her mouth to hide her smile.

Diana's chin went up to a regal angle. ''I don't see anything interesting here,'' she said with a visual sweep of the store.

Tessa drummed up a wide smile. ''We don't try to please everyone, only a select and special type of person.'' Lord, she couldn't believe she'd really said that. Her message was clear.

''Meaning Colby?'' Smoke practically puffed out of Diana's ears. ''You're different. But he'll tire of you quickly,'' she said with a bluntness that was meant to sting.

She could be right, Tessa knew, watching Diana whirl away in a huff.

''Oh, Tessa,'' Marla said on a giggle as the door slammed shut behind Diana. ''She looked furious.''

Tessa thought so, too. She wondered if the woman was worrying needlessly. At one time, Colby had loved Diana, wanted to spend his life with her. They had history, memories. And despite the happiness Tessa had been enjoying with Colby, he'd never said that he wanted anything lasting with her.

''Tessa, can I step outside for a moment?''

She focused on Marla. Through the front window, Tessa saw a man pacing on the porch. The old boyfriend, Tessa knew. That was good news. ''Sure, go ahead.''

She wished her future looked as bright as Marla's.

She could try to peek. No, that rarely worked for her. The future for other people was so much easier to see.

Frowning, she wandered behind a counter. With the ring of the bell, she looked up.

"You're frowning again."

She worked up a smile to match Colby's. "I'm a deep thinker. You smile a lot, you know," she teased.

"Because I'm staring at you."

She skirted the counter to step up to him. "I didn't expect to see you so soon." She couldn't remember a time in her life when she'd felt so happy around someone.

"You must have cast a spell. I couldn't stay away."

Leaning into him, Tessa draped an arm over his shoulder. "Poor Colby."

With an arm at her waist, he tugged her closer. "You need to display more sympathy."

"Hmm. Let me think of a good way." She kissed a corner of his lips. "Like this. Is that what—" At a movement to her left, she paused and angled a look at the opening door.

Her hand out in front of her, Marla rushed to her and flashed an engagement ring at them.

"Oh, Marla!" Tessa met her halfway for a hug. "How wonderful. When?"

"Well." She placed a palm against her flat belly and spoke low to Tessa. "It'll have to be soon. I'm pregnant."

"I'm so happy for you." Peripherally she saw

Colby slowly shaking his head in the manner of someone coming to grips with news.

He, too, offered good wishes before Marla left.

"Told you so," Tessa said when they were alone again.

"I'm not asking how you knew. But I'm surprised you're happy. I thought you didn't like the tool salesman."

"He's not the father. Her old boyfriend is."

He draped an arm around her shoulder, absently rubbed his hand up and down. "She broke off with the tool salesman?"

Tessa leaned into him as he stroked her arm. "All by herself."

"Pleased, aren't you?" With the ring of his cell phone, he gave her a wry grin as he checked the caller ID. "My mom."

Tessa finished unwrapping the last few items in the crate while he talked to Louise, but their conversation was brief.

He came near and lifted a wooden sculpture of a bull's head from the crate for her. "She called to tell me that the woman Harriet helped is in town."

Straightening, Tessa snagged a towel from the top of her desk to wipe off her hands. "The one who left the abusive husband?"

"That one. Where do you want this?" He scowled. "What is this for?"

"Fertility." As he arched a brow, he almost looked as if he was contemplating buying it and hanging it in the stall with Ladyfair. "You need to talk to that woman, find out about her ex-husband, where he is, where he's been."

"That wasn't in my plans. But yeah, I do."

Tessa set down the towel. "Where is she?"

"In a motel nearby. Go with me. She might feel more comfortable talking to a woman."

Tessa didn't hesitate. She'd been useless so far. She'd do anything to help them. "Does your mother think the man may have killed Harriet?" she asked, after giving a few instructions to Marla.

"She's looking for answers anywhere she can, even from this woman, though she's a stranger."

"It's so difficult for these women. They're the really brave ones." She thought again about her vision. "Harriet was shot with her own gun, wasn't she?" she asked after they climbed into his truck.

"That's right. If you need to know the particulars, you could learn them from Chelsea."

"I know them."

Before negotiating a turn onto Main Street, he angled an askance glance at her.

"And a pillow was used?"

"A pillow? Yes, there's a pillow missing. You heard about that?" he asked.

So still he didn't believe. She gave him a strained smile. She'd heard nothing. She'd seen it. "I guess I must have. Did the bruise on her hip match the chair railing?"

He was slow to respond. "It did. They thought she bruised it when—"

"She tried to run."

"Yeah," he said so quietly she barely heard him. "That's right."

* * *

Colby thought about her questions during the drive. Had she talked to Holt or Chelsea? She must have. Otherwise, how could she have known all that? What if she really could see more than other people? She was uncannily accurate about his aunt's death.

He glanced at her. Staring out the window at the passing scenery, she'd been quiet for several minutes. Had she had a vision, seen his aunt's killing and kept that to herself for his family's sake? If she'd seen the killer, he was sure she would have said something. Damn, what did he know for sure? Though he didn't understand anything about psychics, he wasn't so skeptical anymore.

"This motel?" she asked, breaking the silence.

Colby nodded and turned into a parking space. "Unit two."

The woman was thin with long, fair-colored hair. In a bright blue playpen with a duck design, a little one with round cheeks and dark hair cooed while she shook a set of colored keys. "My other kids are in Boston. I didn't want to take them out of school, but I had to come. I'm real sorry about your aunt."

"Thank you." Colby perched on the edge of the desk in the motel room.

Tessa moved closer to the woman, then sat on a chair across from her. "Why did you come?"

"I wanted to talk to Harriet's sister. Your mom, huh?" she asked Colby. "She's a real sweet lady. I wanted her to know how good her sister had been to me. When I was living in Rumor, she came to the trailer court, told me if I needed help, she'd be there for me and my kids. Lenny came home while she was visiting, told her to get the hell out. Harriet stood up to him.''

Colby wasn't surprised. His aunt wasn't easy to know, allowed no one to push her around. He recalled an incident between her and Henry when he'd been mayor. He'd insisted the town couldn't afford to build the new library. Fearless, she'd arrived at the town council armed with books. How could they not give such treasures a decent home? she'd demanded to know. Colby recalled his mother telling him the story over the telephone when he'd been at a rodeo in Colorado. Harriet wouldn't leave the library. Five hours later, everyone agreed that the fund-raising money the townspeople had collected should include funds for the library. Sadly Colby wondered if his aunt's stubborn streak had frustrated someone and caused her death.

''Harriet told him that she'd leave when I asked her to,'' the woman said. ''I was so—well, you know, no one had ever stood up to him like that before or did that for me. He was so drunk. He didn't care what she'd said. He turned around to leave and stumbled down the trailer steps. That's when she said to me, 'You need to leave now,' and I did. I went with her. She drove me to a motel, paid for me and the kids, even got us something to eat and stayed with us till morning.''

Tessa hunched forward. "What happened then?" she asked quietly.

"Harriet knew someone in Boston who'd give me a job. There was a shelter there, and the kids and I stayed there for a while. Once I got enough money, we moved into a place of our own. Harriet did that for me. When I heard she'd died—was killed—" Her voice broke. She bowed her head for a second. "When I heard, I thought about Lenny."

"Would he do it?"

She raised her head slowly. "Yes, he would."

"Has anyone seen him around Rumor?" Tessa asked when they were in Colby's truck. She wished the woman had something that belonged to her ex-husband, something Tessa could touch. But understandably the woman had wanted nothing of his.

"Henry insists a stranger he saw in town a while back might have been the woman's ex-husband."

"Why would he be in town? The woman had left and was living in Boston."

"But he didn't know that. The sheriff's theory is that he might have come to Rumor to see my aunt and learn his ex-wife and kids' whereabouts from her." Colby shrugged. "Dave's looking for anything that might make sense. It's a possibility. If Henry was right."

She, too, knew Henry's reputation for speaking before verifying. She looked up, noticed Colby had driven them to Mystic Treasures. A pang of disappointment swarmed in on her. She'd thought, she'd hoped he'd want to go to the ranch, that he'd want them to be alone. If he was bringing her to the store, wasn't he worried about her anymore? Tessa frowned with her next thought. Had her going to his ranch been only about a couple nights in his bed?

"I bought two."

She snapped herself from more ponderings about her sex life. Imagine. Tessa Madison had a sex life now. "Two of what?" she asked, noticing he'd already shut off the engine.

He held up a bag. "Locks for your doors. I'll install them, and then—"

"And then?"

"We could go back to the ranch."

"But I'll have locks on my doors."

"Okay." He gave her a wicked grin. "I'll install them tomorrow." Shifting on the seat toward her, he cupped the back of her neck.

His breath warmed her face. His lips tempted as they worked slowly over hers. "You're trying to weaken my knees, aren't you?"

A laugh rode on his words. "Am I doing that?"

"With a kiss."

For her sake, Colby believed she'd be better off at the ranch. He thought it was best to avoid someone seeing him leave her house. She had enough trouble without him adding to it.

A ray of sunlight streaked between the slim opening of the drapes. With Tessa curled against him, he would have preferred to stay in bed longer, but seconds ago, the persistent ring of the doorbell had awakened him. Annoyed, he eased off the mattress and snatched his jeans.

In bare feet, wearing only jeans, he padded down the staircase. The last person he expected to see at that time of the morning was the sheriff.

Dave Reingard looked puzzled by his scowl. "I thought you got up at sunrise, Colby."

"Most mornings."

"It's seven o'clock."

"I know what time it is," he said, not veiling his annoyance. "What do you want, Sheriff?"

"Brought you something. Since you're executor of your aunt's estate, you can have these papers now."

Colby accepted the brown accordion folder. "Thanks for bringing these over."

"Sure." He grinned suddenly as he looked past Colby.

Without a glance back, he guessed that Tessa had come down the staircase. He watched Dave turn away. He didn't think the sheriff passed his day gossiping.

"See ya," Dave said over his shoulder.

"Yeah." Colby closed the door and headed for the kitchen. Better Dave had seen Tessa, and not Henry, who'd been Harriet's lawyer. He'd have felt honorbound to tell his good friend Leone about what he'd seen. The woman didn't need more ammunition to put down Tessa.

The smell of coffee brewing greeted Colby when he entered the kitchen. Standing at the counter, Tessa looked up from pouring herself a glass of orange juice while she munched on last night's popcorn. "Did the sheriff say anything?"

Colby shook his head. "He won't spread gossip."

He dropped the folder on the table. Her hair was tousled from sleep and his hands. She gave him a dreamy smile, and he felt the nudge inside his chest again. He liked having her here, too much, he realized. They'd gone into this with an understanding that there would be no promises. He hadn't expected to want any. He still didn't think he wanted them, but he doubted he'd forget the image of her in his robe, sitting at his kitchen table, or how she felt in his arms.

"What's in that?" she asked.

He traced her stare to the folder Dave had brought over. "Harriet's papers." Papers he needed to read.

"You're executor?"

He released a short, mirthless laugh. "I haven't been in charge since the sheriff began his investigation." Ever since his aunt's death, he'd felt frustration. "Everything was closed by court order."

"Patience doesn't come easy, does it?" she teased.

"Never has." He straddled a chair and slipped papers out of the folder. "Insurance policies." He perused them quickly. As expected, his mother was the beneficiary.

Tessa withdrew a white packet. "The deed to her house is here."

Colby held Harriet's last will and testament and a living trust.

"Was the house left to Louise?"

He nodded, distracted as he skimmed another paper. He couldn't help grinning. "Parrish is on his way out."

While Tessa read the information on the document he'd discovered among his aunt's papers, he left the room to finish dressing. She understood his pleasure about the paper he'd found. She was happy for him and Louise. Though his family still bore many unanswered questions, one of their problems was over. Did she feel so good because Colby did? Was that part of loving? Was it being as one with someone, so their joy or sorrows became your own? What would he think if she told him, *I've chosen you, Colby? You're the one I want to be with first—last—forever.*

"Tessa." He ambled into the room buttoning his shirt. "Let's eat in town tonight."

Had he thought of some other place to go? She believed that only being in Harriet's house might incite more positive visions for her, and it was still sealed by the sheriff. "Do you want me to try something different?"

"Is the Calico Diner okay with you?" Stepping near, he absently fingered strands of hair brushing her shoulder. "They have a good pot roast special tonight."

She didn't think that was his reason for choosing

the diner. "Are you going to tell me why we're going there?"

"It'll be crowded, and the town's biggest gossip works there," he said about a waitress known for knowing everything.

"What are you planning?"

He squeezed by her and reached for the coffeepot. "I want you to stop. I don't want you to help anymore."

Was he serious? She'd yet to learn anything new. Possibly she never would. "We haven't learned anything."

"We've learned that the killer is scared." Facing her, he caught her chin to force eye contact. "I don't want the person to get desperate. And we're going to make sure everyone knows tonight that you're not involved anymore."

It's too late, she could have told him. Even if everyone believed that, she'd be unable to switch off her connection to Harriet. She might still see what happened. Tessa said nothing, thought it best for him to believe his plan. She hoped the killer would, too.

Chapter Eleven

After loading one of the horses on a horse trailer and connecting it to his truck, Colby drove Tessa into town. Not wanting her alone at the store, he didn't leave until Marla arrived.

He was on his way to Whitehorn when it hit him that he missed her. He knew what he was feeling went beyond desire or friendship, but he wasn't ready to name it. He only knew that he felt as if his knees might buckle just from looking at her.

Smiling at his thought, he maneuvered the truck onto a dirt road and toward the ranch of a doting father who was convinced his daughter was destined to be next year's champion barrel rider.

By late afternoon, Colby was back in Rumor. Before the police seal was removed from Harriet's house and Parrish got access to the inside, Colby planned to share his news with the man. He detoured to the sheriff's office to see Holt, but he felt impatience stir to find Parrish.

"We'll be taking the police seal off today. I don't need any trouble, Colby." Holt dropped on his desk a flyer about a man wanted for fraud. "Parrish has been hanging around your aunt's place. Stay away from there until I tell Parrish."

"No trouble," Colby assured him. This was the end of it. "But I'm seeing him."

Holt had been right about Parrish still being at the house. He'd planted himself on the top porch step. "I heard the sheriff's getting rid of this seal today," he said as Colby approached. "About time. Now I can get into my home."

Colby paused at the bottom step. "Don't get too comfortable."

"I'm not planning to," he answered, misinterpreting what Colby meant. "I'm selling it. This little bungalow is what Realtors call cozy." He made a face. "I'd be cramped here. But I should get a good price. Then I'm traveling."

Seeing him leave town suited Colby just fine. "We finally agree about something." Colby waved a paper at him. "We found this."

"What's that?"

"Your walking papers. Did it slip your mind that you received annulment papers?"

Parrish swayed slightly. "What are you talking about?"

"Annulment papers," Colby informed him.

Parrish's pained expression made the moment worthwhile.

"You haven't any rights to anything of my aunt's, according to her will and trust."

Parrish released a resigned sigh. "I'd hoped she'd be more generous."

After what he'd put Harriet through, Colby was amazed he expected anything.

"My plans to travel will have to be put on hold now. Cash is an important item for such a venture."

Colby could care less where he went.

"Is this a celebration dinner of sorts?" Tessa questioned when Colby was steering her toward one of the booths inside the Calico Diner.

"As good as. Parrish is out of my parents' lives now." He chose a booth in the station of the buxom redhead with the wagging tongue.

Sitting across from him in the booth, Tessa returned his smile. "I'm glad for Louise's sake." She scanned the walls above the counter and around the diner, a long mobile home with 1950s decor. Walls were adorned with photographs of Elvis, Marilyn Monroe, James Dean and other favorites. "I've always liked the decor in here."

Materializing beside them, the waitress flashed heavily made-up eyes at Colby. "Want the special?"

Colby didn't miss the innuendo, just chose to ignore it. "Tessa?" he asked while he set his Stetson on the booth seat.

She looked up from the menu. "The Golden Oldie Hamburger."

"I'll have the pot roast," Colby said. While the waitress scribbled on her pad, he played out a scene for her. "Tessa, this isn't working. We both know that."

She nodded. "I'm sorry that I haven't been able to help."

"I know you've tried, but you haven't had any visions or anything. Why don't we forget about this? I'll tell the sheriff you're off the investigation." Colby sent an expectant look at the waitress, who hadn't budged from her spot beside their table. "Was there something else?"

"Uh—" She delivered an embarrassed smile as if unsure they'd been aware of her eavesdropping. "Uh, do you want extra onions?"

Tessa responded with a smile. "No, thank you."

"Coffees?"

"Fine," Colby answered.

"It appeared she bought our act," Tessa said when they were alone.

Colby noticed that the redhead had whispered something to two customers and another waitress since she'd left them. As he'd expected, the diner was jammed. Even Holt and the sheriff were there. Across the room, Holt nodded to him. Dave seemed more engrossed in his dinner than the happenings in the diner.

"That's good," Tessa murmured while setting the menu in its chrome holder.

Not so good for her, Colby decided. A woman at the counter stared over her shoulder and smirked. A man near her sneered. He muttered something to Henry, who'd been a regular every Friday for the fish fry since his divorce. Even a stranger at the counter wore a skeptical, snide grin.

Colby read the body language of the people around him. They thought she'd failed, and had expected it. So he got her out of danger but weakened her reputation as a psychic, hindered her acceptance among them. The crowded diner buzzed with conversation. In their eyes, if she failed to find Harriet's killer, that meant she was a fake. He'd brought her more trouble, hadn't he?

"Don't worry so," she said suddenly.

He met her stare. How did she know he was feeling concern for her at that moment? "I wasn't thinking about the backlash that you'd feel when I said you couldn't help."

"You haven't made anyone change their mind about me. The ones who are whispering never believed."

"Tessa! Tessa!"

Along with her, Colby swiveled a look toward the door. A girl of about seven scurried around tables, then threw her arms around Tessa's neck.

"Oh, Rachel." She hugged the girl. "What a wonderful surprise. What are you doing here?"

"I'm with my grandma," she said, drawing back

to look at a heavyset, gray-haired woman who beamed at them as she approached.

Tessa ran a hand over the girl's shiny brown hair and stood to hug the woman. "Mrs. Saires, it's so nice to see you."

"And you." Her eyes slid with curiosity to Colby. Tessa made the expected introduction.

Everyone shifted as the waitress delivered food.

"Well, I won't keep you." Mrs. Saires motioned toward their plates. "You don't need your food getting cold."

"Why are you in town?" Tessa asked.

"I have a sister living nearby. We'd hoped we'd see you, but when we went to your store, you were gone. I'm so glad we ran into you. Rachel wanted to see you so badly," she said, wrapping an arm around her granddaughter's shoulder.

"I hope I'll see you both again soon," Tessa said.

"Us, too." Lovingly the woman ran a hand over her granddaughter's head. "Now we're going to try the claw game by the door."

"Let me go with Rachel," Tessa said.

The woman's smile widened. "She'd like that."

Tessa took the girl's hand and crossed to the game. The glass box was half-filled with stuffed animals.

"She loves children, doesn't she?" the woman said to Colby.

Colby gave the expected nod, but he didn't know a lot about Tessa. Despite their intimacy, she'd kept her past to herself.

"Every time I look at my granddaughter, I know

she's a miracle. And without Tessa, I wouldn't have her today.''

That caught Colby's attention. ''What do you mean?''

''Our family is so grateful to her. We were staying at my sister's in a neighboring town when Rachel disappeared. Without Tessa and her gift, we might never have found her.'' Distress wrinkled her brow. ''I hate how badly she was treated for helping us.''

Colby wanted to know more, but Tessa was returning to the table.

''We won the purple pig,'' she said on a laugh.

Colby waited while the women shared a goodbye. As the woman and her granddaughter headed for the exit, he slid into the booth. ''The grandmother sang your praises.'' When she made much about smoothing out her napkin in her lap, he persisted, ''Are you going to tell me what happened?''

''As you can see, everything worked out well.''

Colby gave her the time she seemed to want. He cut his meat and took a bite. ''She said that people treated you badly.''

Head bent, she concentrated on pouring a puddle of ketchup on her plate. ''People always doubt me. I had a vision about the little girl and went to the police, told them what I'd seen.'' She picked up her hamburger. ''They laughed, said I must have heard about her, dreamed that I thought I saw her.''

''Rachel?''

''Yes, Rachel. Helping is rarely easy.''

Her eyes met his, carried a sadness. In that second,

he sensed she'd endured an enormous amount of rejection.

"I know they didn't understand," she went on. "But I was frightened for her and hounded them to look in a nearby cave. They found her."

"So you saved her?"

Tessa set down her hamburger and wiped a napkin across her greasy fingers. "That's not what they thought. They assumed that I only could have known where Rachel was if I was involved in her disappearance. And they arrested me."

Instinctively his stomach churned with anger for her. He cursed silently the unfairness she faced. He'd witnessed her concern for others like Marla, the children at the hospital, that little girl. She put her heart in front of her to be broken. She gave to others even knowing she might get hurt. "What happened then?" Whatever he believed didn't matter. She believed in her gift, took risks for it.

"I was booked. I spent the night in a holding cell. In the morning when the police were able to talk to Rachel, she said she'd gotten lost after chasing a butterfly. She got cold, so she went into the cave."

He hated what she'd been put through even as he tried to explain how she knew where the little one was, but he couldn't stop himself. He looked for a logical explanation. She'd walked by the cave and considered it dangerous, and with the publicity about the missing little girl, she dreamed about her, remembered the cave. "Rachel cleared you?"

"Yes. And they released me then. They apologized, but said I had to understand that they couldn't figure out how I could know so much about her disappearance unless I was involved. That made sense to me, but I could never know something that might save someone and keep quiet.''

Across the room, the man watched. The latest news about Warren Parrish and an airtight alibi got Parrish off the hook. Too bad. He'd looked like the perfect fall guy.

What about the fortune-teller? The gossip in the diner minutes ago was that she hadn't seen anything. No one believed she really could do any of that supernatural nonsense. Not really. A phony. Everyone called her that. No one believed in her.

Through dinner, Tessa fretted. After their little act in the diner, the reason she and Colby had begun seeing each other no longer existed. Would all she'd found with him be over with the swiftness of someone snapping fingers?

As they stood on the back stairs outside her house, she decided to take control of the moment. They'd been lovers. It made sense that she'd invite him in. ''Stay the night,'' she said, facing him. She sounded sure, but her heart thudded with her uncertainty.

For a moment, as if he needed time to think about it, he was silent. ''If I do, people will know.''

Tessa shifted her stance. Did he really care? People already knew he was involved with her. What did he really mean? Did he want to say good-night, tell her it had been fun and walk away? Feeling suddenly young and vulnerable, she wished the ground would open and swallow her before she made a complete fool of herself. *You always expect too much, Tessa, even when you know better.* "Okay. It's okay if you don't want to come in." She was rambling, making more of a mess of the moment. She swung away, thinking that a quick exit was best.

Before she started up the stairs, he caught her arm, whirled her to him. "Now I think you are crazy." Humor colored his voice. Their faces were close, their eyes level. "Hell, yes, I want to come in."

Her heart pounded even harder. "But you said—"

"If you're not coming home with me, I'm staying."

"I thought when I asked you in and you—"

"Did I say no?" He placed a kiss on the tip of her nose. "Even more now, I don't want you to be alone. We don't know if the person heard yet about what we said in the diner and will believe that little act."

Was this about protecting her, about guilt for putting her in danger? "I have locks now. Courtesy of you." She needed him to declare feelings, she realized. "You don't have to watch over—"

"You're funny." He cut in. A hint of a grin lifted the edges of his lips. "Watching over you is *not* what I had in mind."

Tessa returned a semblance of a smile. She'd been so prepared for him to stop seeing her. "Does that mean you do want to come in?"

"An understatement." Lightly he stroked her

spine. "But people will see me leave in the morning."

Gossip. Was he really worried about it? "I don't care." She meant that. As much as she wanted to belong, she'd never let others dictate how she'd live her life. In a way, she was the free spirit he believed she was because of her vagabond lifestyle. "Do you care?"

On a laugh, he kept an arm at her waist and urged her up the stairs. "Tessa, you should know better. Do you have the keys?"

"In my purse." She hadn't known better. Childhood memories still haunted her, she realized, aware her insecurity stemmed from others breezing in and out of her life without a look back.

"You'd better find those keys."

His light spirit reached her with the sensuous play of his mouth around the shell of her ear. Looking down, she fished in her shoulder bag for the keys. "They're here somewhere."

"Hurry up."

"I'm trying." At the door, she stopped, leveled a look at him. "You're not helping me." She dug around in her purse until her fingers curled over the keys. "Here." She dangled them at him before turning to unlock the door.

"Give them to me." He reached around her. "Whose dumb idea was it to put a lock on this door?" he quipped, slipping the keys from her fingers.

Enjoying herself, she deliberately chose a way to

distract him. Angling a look at him, she captured his lips with her own. With satisfaction, she heard his groan before he pulled his mouth from hers.

"Tessa, jeez." He fumbled with the lock. "I have it," he murmured against her cheek.

She thrilled at his breathless sound. With his palm, he pushed open the door. His mouth on hers again, he nudged her to back up, to step inside.

They stood in the moonlit living room. She didn't care where they were. She wanted to touch. She was eager. She knew his body now, the muscles, the scars from years of rodeoing.

With a kiss that was hard and meant to never be forgotten, as he tugged down the zipper of her dress, she pulled at the buttons on his shirt. Bending away, he cussed to get off his boots. When he straightened, when his mouth closed over hers, she took control. She reached down, brushed the thin line of hair that disappeared into the waistband of his jeans, then yanked at one of the buttons.

Together they worked at them. He murmured something, but words seemed unimportant. He stepped out of the jeans, then in a sweep of movement, he unsnapped her bra. His hands moved to her hips. Slowly he peeled her panties down.

She didn't speak, could barely think when his lips pressed against her navel. She felt the silk brushing her thighs, the warmth of his lips at her groin. Eyes closed, Tessa heard a moan, her own with his mouth's descent to reach her inner thigh.

Emotion flooded her. As she swayed, she clutched

his shoulders for support. His lips again sought her belly, then he drew her down to the carpet, to him. She was a creature of sensation, lost to the mouth closing over a nipple, tugging and sucking at it.

There was nothing beyond this moment. Whatever stood in their way during daylight vanished beneath the glow of moonlight. Passion's heat slithered over her. She caressed the grooved plane of muscle at his stomach, reached for the waistband of his briefs. She shoved at the fabric until it curled at his hips. Then his hands replaced hers to push the cotton down the rest of the way.

Breathless, she opened her eyes to see him ripping open the foil packet. Another moment that seemed like an eternity passed before his mouth came back to hers, before she felt the length of him against her. She needed no enticement, no languid pace.

As he hurried her, she rushed him. Only sensations mattered when his hand skimmed her body, when his fingers reached the delicate skin between her legs. Hot kisses ran over her breasts to her tummy. His touch didn't stroke or soothe, it urged, tempted, enticed.

With his mouth heating her, she thought he might drive her insane. She grabbed at air. As a swift head-to-toe shudder swept through her, she whispered his name. She waited a second, then wrapped herself around him.

Love me. She could have begged him. Every breath drawn, every sigh released was for him. She wanted to believe in something as delicate as love. He was linking her to him with a kiss, binding her to him with his body. When he slipped into her, flesh blended. Her world exploded with the feel of him, the fullness inside her. No patience existed. Bodies slammed at each other, moved with oneness.

Breathless, hot, she squeezed her eyes tight, cupped his buttocks and strained against him. As she'd done the first time, she tried to remember every second, every sensation. She was weak, limp.

When he pressed his face in the side of her neck, he groaned and shuddered. She'd done this to him. She was strong now. As he numbed her to everything but this moment, her body and the feelings he had aroused, she controlled him, too.

A ragged plea slipped from her lips. She wanted. She needed. Need meant more than just the moment. Need meant heartache. *Don't think,* she told herself. *Don't think. Feel. Love him.*

He'd thought he'd never breathe normally again. That was Colby's first thought the next morning. Outside the bedroom window, birds chirped in an oak tree. Even when his breath no longer had come in harsh, uneven gasps, his heart had pounded as if it would burst through his chest. He stared at the slim, feminine hand resting on it. He wondered if she was aware of her power. Days ago, she'd been innocent, uncertain. Now she weakened him with a caress. Lifting her hand, he threaded his fingers with hers. So fragile. So strong. Effortlessly she could make him beg.

"Hi," she murmured.

"Hi, yourself." With fingertips, he stroked her hair and looked around her bedroom. Clearly she loved books, he realized as he scanned the room and noted shelves of them. He narrowed his eyes at a huge wooden statue shaped like a horse's head. "What's that?"

He felt her shift to see where he pointed. "That's from India. It represents good wishes for prosperity."

"Unusual. What about the other things?"

"The screen is a Korean palace screen, and the Buddha belonged to a friend of my mother's whose husband traveled to the Orient often. The Indian painting on cloth is of the joyous lover god Krishna."

"You're a collector?"

"My mother was a lover of art. She acquired whatever she could."

"And you inherited all of it."

"She didn't have much to leave me. A few things."

She'd said the psychic power was a trait passed on to the women in her family. He stared at a photograph of a soft-looking woman with dark hair. She was kneeling on the beach, laughing, and the wind blew her dark hair from her face as she stared at the young girl tucked close to her side. Mother and daughter?

"What are you looking at?"

"The photograph." She looked angelic. Pale with her dark hair, and those eyes that seemed to see so much. "What about your father?" She'd never mentioned him before.

"He left. He couldn't deal with my mother's gift.

He thought he could when he married her, but he couldn't and he left.''

She'd said it all too simply. ''Did you know him?''

''I never met him.''

''What do you mean when you say he left?''

''While we were still living in Rumor when she was pregnant with me. He'd never had enough faith in her.'' She moved her hand to rest on his chest. ''He left us because he couldn't accept her gift.''

Colby frowned at her words. He'd only been thinking about Tessa. He'd never given her parents much thought before this, or what their lives had been like.

''People can be cruel,'' she added. ''Suspicious. Those who knew them shied away, others acted as if my mother was crazy. My father wanted distance. He turned his back on the woman he'd made a vow to love forever. That's when my mother left Rumor with me.''

He measured his next words before speaking. ''Did she carry the hurt?''

Tessa's eyes met his. ''They were wrong for each other. But yes, he broke her heart.''

Had she grown up with a woman who'd been grieving for one man, for a love lost? Had Tessa's mother searched for someone who might understand her, might accept the risks that came with loving her? From Tessa, he'd gotten the impression that had never happened.

Smelling coffee, he realized she'd eased away. He roused himself and wandered into the living room to search for his boots. Last night he and Tessa had started in the living room, shedding clothes there, then had lit candles and made love again before he'd carried her to bed. It took a few minutes to find everything. Buttoning his shirt, he wandered into the kitchen to the sound of her rattling pots behind a cabinet. ''What are you doing back there?''

''I thought I had a waffle iron here somewhere.''

''Never mind. I don't need you to make breakfast.''

With her quick move toward the refrigerator, her plum-colored robe parted, and he caught a glimpse of a slender thigh. He was becoming crazy about her. She looked soft, but she didn't break easily. This was a strong, resilient woman, he knew. People called her quirky. He smiled. Unique described her better.

''Did you find something?'' she asked when he opened the refrigerator door.

''Orange juice.'' Beneath the morning sunlight streaming into the room, her hair shone. ''But where are the glasses?''

Bent over, she looked at him. ''In that cabinet,'' she said, pointing.

With effort, he dragged his gaze away from her backside and directed his attention to the glassware. He had limited choices. A cup from Niagara Falls, a plastic Disneyland glass decorated with cartoon characters, a green plastic sports glass honoring the Houston Astros. He chose the Astros glass, and while sipping the juice opened a pantry door. ''Lord, woman, you're lucky your teeth don't rot.'' He dangled a bag of bite-size candy bars, known for being filled with nuts and caramel.

She flashed him a pearly white smile. "I brush and floss a lot. So did you find something?"

You, he realized. He'd never planned on this much involvement with her, and now he had a difficult time imagining a day without her in it.

"Colby? Did you find something?" she asked in a slow, measuring way as if talking to a young child.

"Not yet." On a shelf above the cabinets were various stoneware pots. He noticed the window herb garden, the tall dried wildflowers stuck in a vase in a corner.

"I have bread and eggs." She met his stare. "I can't find the waffle iron, but we could have French toast."

Was she really going to cook? "I'll make it."

"My kitchen. I'll cook."

With her movement, the V of the robe billowed. Soft, pale flesh enticed. "You can do that?"

Standing on the opposite side of the table, she closed one eye and leveled a withering stare at him. "Be careful or..."

"Or what?" With her playful mood, as she made a move, he took two steps in the same direction to block her.

On a giggle, she skittered the other way. When she rounded the table, Colby lunged for her and caught her at the waist.

Her head thrown back, she smiled impishly. "Is there something else you want?"

Possessively he skimmed fingers down her hip. "I have an idea."

The gray eyes meeting his sparkled with delight and anticipation. "What is it?" she asked while her hand glided over his buttocks.

He nearly groaned. Against his rib, he felt the quick beat of her heart. He wanted to make it race, thunder with excitement and reached down to part the robe with his fingers. "We can conserve water."

As his hand brushed her thigh, she sighed. "I'll wash your back."

They skipped breakfast. He would have liked a leisurely meal with her, but while he was still drifting from the spell she'd weaved over him, she'd scooted off the bed. No man should feel so content, he reflected. Lazily he raised an arm and pillowed the back of his head with it.

"I have volunteer work at one," she called from the bathroom. "And I have to check some new merchandise at the store first."

As much as he wanted to persuade her to join him, he had to leave, too, for the same reason. He'd offered to deliver donated fans. He eased off the bed and dressed. By the time she appeared, he was sitting on the edge of the bed tugging on his second boot. Kneeling on the floor, she rummaged under the bed, offering him a delectable view of her backside in snug jeans. "Is something missing?"

"Shoes."

He spotted one sandal near a bedside table. "Is there a reward for finding them?"

Straightening, she swung a look at him. As he dangled the sandal by a finger, she laughed, then rose on her knees and coiled her arms around his neck. ''Thank you.''

''My pleasure.'' She glowed. Was he imagining that? Maybe. But he wasn't imagining how beautiful she looked. Or how full of emotion his chest felt just from looking at her.

Chapter Twelve

Another five minutes passed before they started down the inside stairs that led to Mystic Treasures. In response to the ring of the bell, Tessa paused on a step ahead of Colby and bent forward to look over the banister and see who was at the door. She saw the crown of Leone's gray head.

"I could stay," Colby said, indicating he'd seen Leone, too.

"No, you can't," Tessa said. "You've played bodyguard long enough." Letting her hand ride the banister, she descended the stairs ahead of him. What could Leone want now? "You need to leave. I'll meet you at the school."

"Tessa—"

She touched his cheek. "I'll be fine."

He muttered something under his breath before stepping around her. In passing, he nodded hello to Leone, then stepped outside.

Leone hadn't responded. She looked so smugly satisfied that Tessa instinctively prepared for a confrontation. Disdainfully the woman's blue eyes flicked over her. "You're more foolish than I thought if you think for a moment that he believes in your nonsense. Colby Holmes comes from sensible stock. He'd never take up with the likes of you."

Tessa drew a hard breath, a calming one, and ignored what Leone said. "Is there something you want?"

Leone's back went rigid. "Ignore my advice. I could care less," she said. "However, you won't be able to ignore my news. I came to tell you that the town council will officially notify you that your operating license is suspended," she said snidely.

Tessa felt her heart sink to her stomach. Leone had made good on her threat to close her business. Could she appeal to the town council? "Mrs. Burton, you can't—"

"I have," she said firmly. "Don't bother trying to convince me we shouldn't do that. I insisted we should after what I saw last night."

"Last night?" She was confused. "What do you think you saw?"

"I told them that you were holding séances here."

Nothing she said would have surprised Tessa more. "I—I was—what?"

"I saw all the candles last night. In an upstairs

window. Henry, too, saw them from the sidewalk. We knew what you were doing."

"You don't know anything," Tessa said, growing annoyed. With candles flickering, she and Colby had been holding each other in the afterglow of their love-making.

A smug, self-satisfied look settled on the woman's face. "I know that you no longer are a part of this community."

Colby returned to the ranch. He hadn't liked the idea of leaving her to face Leone, but he couldn't insist on staying. He had no right. No strings. No promises. That's what he'd wanted. Simple words. Simple concept. That had been true before, but it wasn't true anymore.

Looking for some way to help her, he stepped into his study and called Holt about checking with florists in Boise. They both doubted they'd learn who'd sent the dead flowers to Tessa, but Colby spent the next hour making the phone calls. No one had made a delivery to Rumor.

After finishing the calls, he strode to the stable. It was good for him to be close to the horses. He'd been so distracted lately because of the investigation and Tessa that he'd felt detached from his ranch and the animals.

This ranch hadn't been bought on a whim. He'd been striving to have the best horse ranch in Montana. He'd thought it would be a legacy to his children. That had been before the breakup with Diana. Now another woman occupied his mind. Now what he'd once considered didn't seem so out of reach.

Before he returned to town, it was afternoon. He joined Garrett in the school parking lot and hefted boxes of fans onto the bed of a pickup truck. Garrett worked while carrying on a conversation with Henry's brother. Colby had his own distraction as he spotted Tessa carrying boxes from the school's gymnasium to her van. Since they'd arrived, they'd been busy and apart. He couldn't help wondering what Leone had felt so compelled to tell Tessa that she'd come into her store.

"You're useless when she's around, you know."

Colby laughed at Garrett's gibe. "It's no worse than you when the cute blond waitress from Whitehorn is around." He tapped Garrett's shoulder, then meandered toward Tessa. As he sidestepped Henry, he heard him expounding about the speed limit outside town being too slow and found himself face-to-face with Parrish. "You're still around?"

Parrish plastered a phony smile on his face. "Always good to see you."

It didn't matter to Colby that evidence proved Parrish had nothing to do with Harriet's death. Colby figured the man had done enough damage when Harriet had been alive. He'd made her life miserable.

"Thought you might like to know. Since I have nowhere else to go, I'll be staying around for a while."

Colby stepped to the side. "Stay away from my

family." Under his breath, he muttered a few choice words. He moved at a slower pace than usual to cool down before reaching Tessa. "Is that van packed full?"

She turned, her ponytail swinging with her movement. Dressed in jeans, a T-shirt and a Houston Astros baseball cap, she looked cute. "Almost."

The smile wasn't in her eyes. He couldn't think of anything or anyone who'd steal it from her except another threat or Leone Burton. He took a guess. "Did Leone cause you much trouble?"

"She came to remind me that lighting candles is forbidden in Rumor."

"What?"

She waved a hand. "What she said can't be changed. So let's not spoil the day."

He wanted to probe. He wanted to tell her she could lean on him, give him her problems. But while she might give her body to him, something made her keep a part of herself from him. "I'll help you deliver."

"Don't you have a list of your own?"

Colby tapped fingers on the ponytail. "You can help me."

"How many go here?" he questioned when they parked outside a couple of rambling ranch homes located on a stretch of well-manicured lawns.

Staring at her list, Tessa walked with him to the back of the van. "Snyder Nursing Home. Five go here."

They delivered them and three large ones to one of the churches for its Sunday service, then drove to the vet's office. Standing by his truck beneath an afternoon sun, Colby felt sweat streaming down the side of his neck. The heat wave had gotten worse. Meteorologists had forecast a record high for the day. Colby had lost count of how long the area had gone through the heat wave. Too long. Too damn long.

"Did you finish those deliveries?" Tessa asked from steps away.

"Done with those. Are you?"

"I took enough into Dr. Hunt's to keep his furry patients happy."

How could she look so cool? He was sweating his butt off, and her skin had only a slight sheen. She looked irresistible. Damn, he had it bad. He wanted to draw her into his arms, kiss her. He couldn't be within two feet of her and not want her. He'd laughed and smiled more since he'd begun seeing her than in a long time. He woke up in the morning simply wanting to see her. He sounded nuts even to himself. Or maybe the impossible had happened. When he hadn't expected it, he'd found her. And he'd fallen in love.

"Doing all that work made me hungry," she said, cutting into his thoughts.

"Hungry?" He gave her his most lecherous look. "For what?"

Tessa laughed. "You're so bad." She gave him an ineffectual punch in the arm. "I have such a craving for teriyaki chicken."

He grinned, loving every quirk in her. "You had almond chicken a couple of days ago."

"I could eat that for breakfast."

"You're kidding, aren't you?"

"Why is that so hard to believe? Do you sometimes have eggs for dinner?"

"Don't get logical on me."

"Egg foo yung," she said. "That's an omelette."

"You've got a weird stomach, woman."

"Weren't you warned that I was weird?"

He kissed the side of her neck. "Unusual."

"Some people might say peculiar."

"Or rare," he murmured, skimming her arm.

"You're very distracting." She motioned toward the delivery sheet in his hand. "Who else is on your list?"

"A rancher. Clarence Harmon needs fans for his livestock."

"I'll meet you there. I have to deliver fans to the Raymonds' ranch. Mrs. Raymond, Ruth, thinks I can give her spiritual guidance about when to plant her tulips." He smiled with her, but Tessa could tell that he thought she was teasing. "You think I'm fooling, don't you? Astral planes and cosmic energies and seeing into the future are part of my life."

"I don't care about the future," he returned. "What matters to me is this moment—you." He slid a hand around to the back of her neck and held her face still. He kissed her long, thoroughly. "What you make me feel," he whispered close to her mouth.

So badly Tessa wanted to believe in them. Desperately she wanted to believe in them, believe she'd finally met someone who could really love her. She wanted to believe she could have forever with him.

But their time was limited. With Leone's threat, there seemed no point in unpacking merchandise. She'd have to leave. She could reopen elsewhere or sell her merchandise. There was a New Age store in Oregon. She'd met the owner at a psychic fair. Perhaps he'd buy everything.

She'd planned to keep the problem to herself. She wished she could tell Colby about Leone's visit, but it was best to keep him out of everything.

For forty-five minutes, she visited with Ruth Raymond, who'd become a regular at her store. According to Ruth, the top gossip in town was about Tessa and Colby. Tessa sidetracked her with information about planting the bulbs. She couldn't answer any of the woman's questions, especially one about a wedding in the future. "I can't see my own future," she simply answered.

By the time she reached the Harmon ranch, she'd tucked away any youthful fantasies about orange blossoms and wedding bells, about staying in Rumor, raising children here.

She parked her van and slid out from behind the steering wheel to wait for Colby. "All my deliveries are made," she said as he approached with Clarence Harmon.

Though Tessa smiled at the rancher, he remained stone-faced. "Heard you delivered fans to the Raymonds. Ruth believes in that nutty stuff at your store, doesn't she? If you ask me, it's all nonsense. You're like your mother, aren't you?''

"You knew her?''

"Everyone thought she was crazy," he said with candor more than malice. "Lots of people thought your father would marry another woman.''

Tessa felt tension in Colby's hand on her back. Had people asked her father why he was with the crazy woman? Would they say that to Colby if he kept seeing her?

Annoyance hung in Colby's voice. "Guess people were wrong about a lot of things," he said pointedly.

The rancher's frown deepened. "Didn't mean any offense, Colby.''

"Glad to hear that." Gently he pressed her back and urged her toward their vehicles, but Tessa sensed his anger. "Don't let him upset you," he said after they'd stepped away.

"I'm okay," she assured him. "Not everyone accepts what I can do. I know that." Not even Colby, she thought sadly.

In her van, she flicked on the CD player while she drove to Colby's ranch. Like Harmon, a lot of people would never accept her. That rancher had made her remember how difficult it was for her mother and Tessa to gain acceptance, to belong. Colby had always known the feeling of belonging. With the trouble Leone was about to drop in her lap, if she stayed in Rumor, kept seeing Colby, people would begin to treat him differently.

* * *

Colby was glad to be alone in the truck with time to think. He drove to the school and turned in the delivery lists with the recipients' signatures on them. He avoided small talk with Pierce, wanted to head for the ranch. He'd expected Tessa to be home. *Home.* His thought stirred a frown. *It's my home,* he reminded himself, *not hers.* But it didn't have to be that way.

When he made the turn onto the dirt driveway and saw her van parked by the house, a sense of contentment came over him. He wanted her near—always, he realized.

He'd felt not only passion but also love when he'd held her. He'd believed he wouldn't want love again, and then he'd met her.

Parked, he climbed out of the truck, cast a look around him. He had plenty to offer if she wanted it. Would she? he wondered as he started for the house.

He took a step, but stilled in response to the sound of a car engine. Raising a hand, he tipped his hat to shade his eyes from the glare of the sun and squinted at the car parking behind his truck. He knew who it was before the woman slid out of the shiny red sports car.

Smiling, Diana slammed the door of her Corvette. "Colby, you've been avoiding me. I came by the other evening, and you weren't home." Looking as if she'd stepped off the pages of some fashion magazine for the best-dressed look at a dude ranch, she ambled to him.

With every breath, he drew in her fragrance. And he felt nothing. Long ago, he'd stopped caring. He knew that now. He'd let feelings stymie him, keep him from going on with his life.

"Colby, we need to spend time together." Possessively she placed a hand on his chest. "Remember how good we were together?"

He remembered that she'd left him believing marriage was for other people.

"I was wrong before."

He raised a hand to block hers from touching his face, held it for a second. Hurting her in any way wasn't a part of his plan. "No, it's over."

"Why should it be? You aren't still sulking about what happened before, are you?"

He hadn't thought about her, about that time since meeting Tessa. "That has nothing to do with this. We both know that it's over."

Her brows made a small frown. "The only reason you'd say that to me is because there's someone else." Her voice trailed off as she glanced sidelong at Tessa's van. Incredulity raised her voice. "It's because of the weird little palm reader, isn't it? She's hardly your type, Colby."

"Could be that she's exactly my type."

"You're serious?" She looked at him as if he'd lost his mind. "Have you told her that you love her?"

He hadn't. Not yet. "You'd never be happy here, Diana."

What sounded like both annoyance and anger edged her voice. "So that's it?" When he didn't answer, she shook her head at him. "You'll be sorry, Colby." When she whirled away, he didn't expect her to look back, but she paused at her car door. "She isn't right for you."

He figured Diana would be upset for fifteen minutes, then start planning where to go to find some excitement. She'd told him she considered Rumor a hick town. In time, ranch life would have bored her. He knew they'd have never been happy together.

A step from the porch, he looked up. Tessa stood before him with her carryall on her shoulder. Black and silver earrings dangled almost to her shoulders. The gauzy white top, the squash blossom belt, and long floral skirt gave her a Gypsy look. "Where are you going?"

"I have to handle some business."

"What?" Something in her eyes stilled him, stopped him from smiling.

"She wants you back, doesn't she?"

If she'd seen them talking, she must have also seen the irritation in Diana's stride when she'd walked away. This wasn't about Diana. So what was wrong? Didn't she realize by now he was there for her? *If you have a problem, tell me,* he wanted to say. "She's part of my past."

"Is she?"

"She was even before I met you, Tessa." But he'd been too dumb to realize what he knew now. "You'd have known that if I'd told you the truth about Diana and me."

Interest swept into the gray eyes that had weakened his resistance since the moment they'd met. "The truth?"

He had to level with her, should have before this.

"Everyone believed Diana and I agreed to end our engagement. The gossipers had insisted we were perfect for each other." He stepped closer, needing nearness with her. "The truth was she dumped me." He'd thought it would be harder to share that with someone. But Tessa wasn't just anyone. It occurred to him that he trusted her more than anyone else. "She found something better. She met her late husband."

Empathy softened her eyes. "Colby." She touched his hand. "Colby, you don't have to go on."

She'd shared hurt about her father, about some guy who'd let her down. "You need to know it all. Rich, older, he lavished her with expensive gifts. Suddenly I was just a rodeo man. I made good money, but I couldn't afford to give her the same kind of things."

Her hand fell to her side. "But now she doesn't need you to. She's a rich widow. She has the money."

"Yeah, that's true."

"And she wants you."

Colby grinned wryly. There was too much truth in what she'd said. "I wasn't good enough before."

"Now you can have her."

"Tessa, none of this has anything to do with her. Don't you know that? This is about me. About pride. She bruised the hell out of it when she rejected me. I was convinced I wouldn't let any woman do that to me again."

"Oh." Tessa's heart twisted. Here was his pain. She opened herself to it, to the grief, to his embarrassment, felt all of it. She realized in that moment what he'd just given her. He'd opened his soul to her.

He'd told her something that had hurt him badly. No man had ever given her so much.

"I want to be with you all the time."

Her heart skipped. She wanted that, too. She'd love to say yes, but for both their sakes, she couldn't. "Oh, Colby, you're not being sensible."

He laughed at her words. "Don't you be," he said, wrapping his arms around her.

She was so open to him, to his feelings. Emotion welled within her. She felt his sincerity, his caring. Desperately she wanted to believe in them, believe she'd finally met someone who could really love her, someone she could be with forever.

"I know you've been hurt. But give us a chance."

She frowned, heard his voice. But his words grew softer. She stared at him, saw his mouth moving, but she slipped into a silent world.

With a shudder, she jerked back. *Flames shot up in front of her face.* An oppressing heaviness descended on her so quickly, she lost a breath. She shook her head, tried to block the image. *She sucked in a breath, coughed. A crackling thundered in her ears. Heat. The heat swarmed in around her, beaded her brow, her upper lip, bathed the back of her neck. Fire licked at her feet, her hands.*

The flames teased the branches of towering trees around her. She was in the woods. Fire raged around her. As the acrid smoke closed in on her, her eyes smarted. She raised her hands to shield her face against the blast of heat. "Fire!" Run. She whirled to escape the smoke and flames. They were everywhere.

Panic seized her. She couldn't breathe. No air. Coughing, she struggled for her breaths. "Fire! Fire!"

"Tessa!"

She jerked, gasped for breath. Hands on her upper arms tightened, shook her.

"Tessa, what fire?"

Her heart racing, she stared at the male face. A moment passed before her mind registered that it was Colby's.

"Tessa! What fire?"

"In the woods. There's a fire," she yelled. "At the edge of your property."

She looked up, searched his eyes for only an instant. Disbelief lived in their darkness. She couldn't wait. He wasn't listening, wasn't believing. She didn't have time to convince him. Angry, she hit a palm against his shoulder to push past him.

Before she could take another step, he snagged her arm.

Tessa spun and punched his shoulder. "Leave me alone." Frantically she twisted away from him to get free. "You don't believe. Fine. Stay," she yelled.

"Get in the truck," he shouted, freezing her to the spot.

Uncertain, she stared at him.

"Get in the damn truck!"

With him, she raced for it. He said nothing while he drove. Sitting beside him, Tessa listened to him calling in the fire on his cell phone.

He finished the call, veered right hard and took her on a jostling drive over a road full of potholes and ruts. He'd alerted emergency services, was acting on faith alone. If they went there and there was no fire, he'd look the fool.

In the distance, she heard the wail of sirens. They neared the woods to see a fire crew scurrying down a ravine. Tessa saw the flames, the hazy smoke graying the sky and mantling the trees.

Behind a fire engine, Colby braked the truck to a skidding stop. She jumped out in unison with him and ran forward.

Trucks and cars of townspeople who were with the volunteer fire department barrelled down the country road toward them. Tessa watched as hoses were unrolled.

Near a fire engine, the town's fire chief issued an order. "Who called it in?" he asked then.

"Colby Holmes," someone said.

The man shot a look at Colby. "Damn! Good job, Colby."

He responded with a strained smile. *He's uncomfortable,* Tessa realized. Was he wishing he hadn't been the one who called in the fire? She stepped back to put more distance between them.

"How did he know?" someone asked.

"Tessa Madison. She saw."

People were whispering about her, about him. Tessa glanced his way. He hadn't looked at her since they'd arrived.

Chapter Thirteen

She could handle the stares. She'd been stared at before. But could he? She'd always believed there was no certainty about love or marriage for someone like her. She'd seen the hint of doubt in Colby's eyes when she'd told him about the fire. He could claim her psychic ability didn't bother him, but he'd left the rodeo to have a normal life. He'd stopped taking risks, wanted a safe life.

He'd never have one with her. She couldn't be the one to take everything away from him, and she would. With her, life carried risks, risks that she'd see something so strong, so disturbing, she'd have to beg others to listen. And his normal life would change forever.

"I'll meet you back at the ranch later," he said, touching her arm. "I need to stay here."

She had to make the move now. "I'll be leaving, Colby."

"All right." Distracted, he noted where the other volunteer firefighters were heading. "I'll stop by the store."

"No, you don't understand." Her throat felt tight. "I'm going back to Texas."

A second, no more, passed. He turned to her. "What are you talking about?"

"I'm closing the store." He didn't need to know more, know she was being forced out. "Nothing is working out." But then she'd always known it wouldn't. Life with her wouldn't be normal. They'd have bad moments.

"Just like that you're closing it?" he snapped. "What about us?"

It hurt to say the words. "We weren't meant to last." Another woman, one who could give him a more stable world, wanted in his life again.

The anger flared. "What was this, then?"

Chaos surrounded them. She'd chosen the moment wisely. He had no time for her right now. That was best. She couldn't listen to him, couldn't let herself weaken beneath words she wanted to hear. She saw his confusion, but couldn't help if she wasn't making sense to him. She needed to break away. She didn't ever want him to be hurt, to lose everything because of her. And despite what he'd said, he was uneasy about her gift. "I—need to leave," she said as firmly as she could when all she wanted to do was fall into his arms. "You saw how people acted."

He spoke quietly, calmly, as if suddenly aware of the people around them. "Who cares?"

She glanced around them, knew some people were watching. "You might."

He reached out, but with her slight step back, didn't touch her. "You don't think very much of me, do you?"

Tessa knew how people would react. Until they talked to him, learned she was with him, they might think she'd started the fire. She could imagine Leone yelling, "Witch," to anyone who'd listen. "I know it's not easy to live with all of this."

"Who are we talking about?" His jaw tightened. "Me or that guy Seth?"

Tessa's heart hammered. "He has nothing to do with us." She meant that. Often Colby had tried to understand. This really wasn't about Seth. It was about not hurting the man standing before her.

"But you think I'm like him."

"I think you believe you'll keep feeling the same but—" How much she wanted to believe in them. He offered everything she'd always wanted. Stability. Predictability. A place to call home. And she was everything he didn't need. An ache knotted her throat. There were no guarantees that one day he wouldn't change his mind, wouldn't want the normal life he could have with Diana. "I know what can happen. I'll bring risks into your life."

"I'm used to them." Again he looked away, seeming torn by a responsibility and the need to finish talking to her.

That's what she'd wanted. If he had time to convince her, she might believe in them. "I think what I do scares you."

For a long moment, he was quiet as if aware she spoke the truth. "I'll admit that I don't understand it," he said honestly.

Tessa looked past him as one of the firefighters came up beside him. "Colby, are you staying to help?"

An ache for the love she was losing pierced her, threatening tears. Before she succumbed to selfishness and let herself believe what wasn't possible, she whirled away.

"I'll be there," Colby answered, dealing with annoyance at being interrupted. He battled the feeling to keep from unfairly venting at the guy. "Give me a few minutes. Tessa—" He turned to her, but she was gone. Colby cursed. Why did she have so little faith in them?

Because you do, he told himself. He'd seen hurt in her eyes. She'd wanted one thing from him earlier. She'd wanted him to believe in her. At the moment she told him about the fire, he hadn't been sure he ever would.

"She's kind of spooky," an old-timer standing nearby said to a buddy. "How did she do that?"

"I'm real glad she did," the other guy said.

Colby had seen the stares, as if there was something wrong with her. People made her sound strange. Alien. He wasn't sure about what had happened. He didn't understand it. But he knew she'd felt that fire. And most of all, he knew what he felt for her.

He donned hard hat and gloves, and grabbing a shovel, he joined the others. Falling in line between two neighbors, he began digging a trench, a firebreak, through the woods to the road.

For a few frightening moments, she'd gone rigid, her eyes wide, then she'd started screaming at him. When he'd touched her, she'd felt hot, feverish. A dozen thoughts had barraged him. He'd gone through a second of doubt. Only a second. Then he'd seen the fear in her eyes.

Colby threw another shovelful of dirt down. The whirl of a helicopter grabbed his attention. It and an aerial tank circled overhead, dropped fire-retardant chemicals on the blaze. Smoke engulfed the planes. The smell of the fire covered the volunteers and the firefighters. Nearby a crew felled a tree with electric saws to prevent the fire from jumping across the road.

By midnight, a hue of red warmed the night sky. Lights on the firefighters' helmets shone on the silhouettes of trees. Smoke billowed in the night sky like a dark gray cloud.

Hours later, Colby's back ached. Exhaustion seeped into him. Soot smudged his face and the faces of the men around him. But they'd reached the end of the road. As he brushed sweat and grime from his face, word came down the line that the fire had been contained.

He straightened, squinted against the morning sunlight and relinquished his shovel to another volunteer as a shift change occurred.

"'Twas to be expected with this heat," firefighters commented to anyone listening.

"Got lucky on this one," Colby heard someone say.

In passing, he received a pat on his back. "Sure was good you called when you did, Colby."

Beneath the canvas gloves, blisters had formed. He yanked off the gloves, stared at the raw flesh. "I'm not the one to thank." He'd take a shower, catch a few hours' sleep, then go see Tessa.

"I heard that. Could say she's a hero."

Another man nearby grunted. "Could say."

Grudging acceptance. Tessa would be satisfied with that for now. And in time, people would see past what they viewed as odd. They'd learn about the woman who brought smiles to the faces of sick children, who gave up time to help the townspeople whatever way she could. They'd learn what he knew. She was special.

After showering and dressing, he drove toward town.

He didn't bother to sleep, was running on adrenaline, trying to come up with the right words to convince her that he wasn't a jerk. He'd let her down, he knew. Sure he'd called in the fire, driven to the site, but he'd struggled with disbelief. And she'd seen that. Then she'd heard people and their words, spooky, weird. She'd expected the worst and had walked away from him because she didn't think he was strong enough.

He braked in front of Mystic Treasures, uncertain what to say to her. What words would reach her? She'd been hurt by two men who should have loved her more. How did he convince her that he wasn't like either one of them?

Oh, hell, he was, wasn't he? He halted before taking another step. What happened between Tessa and him was his fault. She'd needed to know he loved her, and he'd never said the words. He'd let Diana do a real number on him, he realized. Because of some dumb thinking, he'd never told Tessa that he loved her. No wonder she doubted that he'd stick around if the going got tough.

Without enthusiasm, Tessa pushed the broom around the storeroom floor. When she'd awakened, she'd considered burying her head beneath the pillow until the ache within her had subsided. On legs that had felt like lead, she'd moved out of bed, showered and dressed. But nearly three hours had passed since then. She managed thin smiles for customers, mumbled a few words to Marla before her assistant took off for her breakfast at Lou's grocery store, a one-story white building that was a combination grocery and drugstore.

She hated the thought of telling Marla the store was closing. A lump settled in Tessa's throat as she looked around her. She didn't want to give up the store. She didn't want to move away. She just wanted to curl up somewhere and cry.

Love for Colby filled her. She'd never thought she'd find love, never expected the happiness she'd known with him. She'd wanted to hold on to it, and her love for him, but if he kept being with her, one day he'd have to defend her, face ridicule for being with her. She couldn't be the one to take friendships and a sense of belonging away from him.

In a rush, Marla burst into the store. She dangled a bag from Lou's. Tessa assumed it was her usual apple Danish. "Tessa!" Excitement raised her voice an octave. "Everyone is talking about you."

She'd expected that. She'd done something yesterday that had forced her gift in everyone's face. No hiding anymore.

"You're a hero. Or is that a heroine? No, I think you're a hero."

Tessa raised her head. "People aren't saying I'm weird?"

"You aren't weird, just different," Marla returned lightly.

Marla made her smile despite the sadness shadowing her. "Thank you."

"Well, you are different. But good different. And everyone knows that now."

It all sounded too easy to Tessa.

"Everything is going so well. I'm so happy for you." She gave Tessa a hug. "And you have Colby, too. This is almost like a fairy-tale ending, Tessa."

Hardly. She'd lost her store, her livelihood. She'd

have to move. She hated to burst Marla's romantic bubble, but Tessa couldn't let her go on about Colby. It hurt too much to think about him. "Marla, I'm not seeing Colby anymore."

"Why?" Marla's voice was troubled. "I know what I saw, Tessa. With these," she said, pointing at her eyes. "He's crazy about you. He can't keep his hands off you. He—"

"Is gone," Tessa said with feigned calmness. She eyed a love potion. If only it could be sprinkled on someone and make everything right.

"I think you're wrong," Marla said from behind her.

Tessa pivoted, determined to be firm with her friend. Her first thought was that she was imagining he was there, leaning against the doorjamb. In a heart-beat, her mind betrayed her with wishful thoughts about love and forever.

An instant later, she wanted to yell at Colby to go away. Didn't he understand that she was trying to protect both of them from more hurt? After struggling all night to convince herself that she'd been right to break away, she felt confused and uncertain. She drew a deep breath, emotionally seesawing between a yearning to yell and a longing to cry. Most of all, she wanted to step into his arms.

What did it matter what she felt? She couldn't make him love her and she couldn't settle for less. She couldn't stand to give everything of herself, love him, then be left. She didn't want to be hurt as her mother had been. She didn't want to believe in love and learn she never had it. "I didn't expect to see you."

"I came to get my palm read," Colby said.

"You don't believe in such things."

"That's what we need to talk about." Behind him, the bell above the door rang. Under his breath, he cursed before he turned to see the customer.

Looking as displeased as ever, Leone entered the store.

"I'll wait on her," Marla volunteered.

Tessa reached out and touched Marla's arm to stop her. "She isn't here to buy anything." Could the day get worse? Tessa wondered. What could she want now?

Leone's eyes shifted from Colby to Tessa. "I was told that you no longer are helping with the investigation about Harriet Martel's murder."

"No, I'm not."

"Is there something you want to know?" Colby asked Leone.

"No." She faced Tessa. "I would like to talk to you." Her chin lifted to a superior tilt as she looked Colby's way. "Alone."

He didn't look fazed by her dismissal or inclined to move.

Tessa swept an arm toward the storeroom. She'd tried to measure the woman's mood, but felt only the usual hostility. "We can talk in there."

Colby raised a halting hand. "Never mind. I'll do some crystal gazing."

Leone scowled after him. "He isn't serious."

Tessa couldn't help smiling. That was so Colby. He'd chosen a deliberate way to side with Tessa. Oh, she didn't doubt he meant well, wanted her. But no ordinary feelings from a man worked for her. They hadn't for her mother, either. Tessa knew what she needed. She needed a strong man, a strong love.

Looking uncertain, Marla hovered at the storeroom doorway before disappearing into the room.

Leone cleared her throat, demanded Tessa's attention. "I learned that you alerted everyone about the fire," she finally said, obviously satisfied with their privacy. "Townspeople are grateful. Several of the town council members opposed my efforts to close your store."

It took a moment before her words sunk in, before Tessa realized what Leone was really saying. Some people didn't want her gone. Though she doubted that would change the final outcome, she felt good in knowing a few people were on her side.

"They're of no mind. I have enough influence to override them, but I believe in returning favors," Leone said grudgingly.

"Favors?" Despite Tessa's confusion, a thread of hope quickened her heart.

"I've come to tell you that I won't persist in trying to close your store. What's best for this town matters most to me."

Tessa was dumbfounded. She hadn't thought anything would change Leone's mind. She swept a look around her, absorbed everything in the room. She'd be able to stay. Maybe she'd even make more friends, if what Marla had said was true. Her gaze shifted to Colby. No, she couldn't stay. Never would she hurt him, but she wanted Leone to know what she felt. "Mrs. Burton, I don't want to harm this town." Tessa waited for the woman's eyes to meet hers. "I don't understand why you're so angry with me. We hardly know each other."

"I knew your mother," Leone said crisply. "You look a great deal like her."

My biggest sin, Tessa mused. *But why?*

"I knew your father, also."

"My father?" That was news. "You knew him?"

"Do you really expect me to believe that you didn't know about us?"

Tessa was baffled. "I'm sorry. *Us?*"

A brittleness tinged Leone's voice. "I assumed your mother would tell you, brag how she was the one he chose, that he walked away from me for her."

A sick feeling settled in Tessa's stomach. She recalled the rancher's words about everyone thinking Tessa's father would marry some other woman. Leone. That woman had been Leone.

"I was the one Steven was engaged to." As if alone, she stared with distant eyes. "Do you know what it's like to have the man you love walk away from you?"

How ironic, Tessa mused. Her father had done just that to her mother, too. But no one knew. And here was Leone admitting that as a young girl, madly in love, she'd felt the same emotion her mother had because of the same man.

"She used her strange way on him," Leone said. "It was her fault that I lost the most wonderful man in the world. And then your mother didn't even appreciate him. When she tired of him, he was so humiliated that he left town."

Tessa was stunned. Leone really believed that Cassandra had taken her love away from her, and when Cassandra had tired of him had sent him out of her life. No one knew he'd left her. No one knew that he'd been a weak man.

Tessa remembered Louise's comment about her mother being restless, wanting to travel. What she'd really wanted was a home and family. Abandoned by her husband, she'd left Rumor. She'd let people believe that she was dissatisfied with her life in Rumor rather than let them learn she'd been deserted.

"You're like her. I know you are."

Tessa felt so sad suddenly. After all these years, the woman still carried the hurt and heartache of that first lost love, still was looking to blame someone and unfairly had chosen Tessa's mother. How wrong Leone was about Tessa's father.

Leone believed Tessa's mother had been guaranteed the love of her life because of her gift. But there were no guarantees in love.

Tessa looked away from Leone's tight-lipped expression. Colby stood by the crystal balls, turning one in his hand. Oh, how silly she'd been. "I'm sorry you feel that way, Mrs. Burton. But yes, I am like her," she said honestly.

Tessa faced her own dragon. Most of her adult life, she'd worried she'd lose at love just as her mother had. She'd wanted a guarantee that Colby would love her forever. Rather than risk the kind of rejection her mother had felt, rather than take a chance at happiness, she'd turned away from him. She'd worried so much that, when he'd offered her everything she wanted, she was too afraid to believe in it.

"Did she give you more trouble?" Colby's voice broke through her thoughts.

Lost in them, she'd been unaware Leone had left. Tessa watched the door closing behind her. "No." Even as she craved to feel his arms around her, she stayed rooted to the spot. "She's leaving me alone."

"That's good."

Desperately she searched for something to say. "Is there any news about the investigation?"

"No. But I'm not giving up. We'll find Harriet's killer."

Tessa wished she'd given him the name of the person. "Is the fire out?" she asked to prevent an uncomfortable silence.

"Almost." He stepped closer, touched her arm. "Because of you." He frowned. "I didn't understand, Tessa. I didn't believe. I do now."

Tessa was speechless. Words she'd never expected him to say quickened her pulse.

"And you might not believe this right now, but you will in time. I will always believe in you."

She could hardly breathe. He really believed in her. She saw the truth in his eyes.

"I love you, Tessa." He moved a hand to her waist. Though his touch was light, she felt tension in his fingers. "I love everything about you. I love just being with you."

Tears came to her eyes. No one had ever said such words to her. A dream she'd carried with her all her life was within reach. She released an astonished laugh as tears fell. This was all she'd ever wanted. "I love you, too." His lips silenced her, meeting hers with a kiss so gentle and loving that she swayed into him.

"I'm sorry," he whispered against her mouth. "All that's happened between us is my fault."

Tilting her head, she shook it. "No, it wasn't. I've had a hard time believing in you because so many people never believed in me. I saw how hurt my mother had been because the person she loved the most had turned his back on her and left."

"Your father?"

"Yes." She placed her hand on his chest, felt the steady beat of his heart. "The heartache was always a part of us. My mother always seemed so lost. I never wanted to feel that way, to let a man leave me.

He abandoned us, Colby. He simply got up one day and walked out of her life.''

"And you thought I'd do the same thing.''

Breathing seemed difficult. "I thought if I left first that you'd be happier.''

"I'm supposed to be happier without you?'' He tugged her close again. "Wrong. Since I met you, this is the first time you've said something batty. Astral planes, cosmic energies, charms and crystal balls all make sense in their own way. This doesn't.''

"But it wasn't about you.'' She coiled her arms around his neck, not thinking about anything except how much she needed him. "That's what I realized. I only convinced myself it was. It was all about me. I've been afraid.''

"You had good reason,'' he said understandingly. "You've been ridiculed and rejected. You needed reassurances. I never said the words you needed to hear. A bruised pride made me hold back. No more. Tessa—'' He paused, frowned and looked down with the ring of his cell phone.

"You're ringing.''

Reverently he brushed strands of hair from her cheek. "Forget it.''

She couldn't help smiling. "No. You need to answer the call.''

His eyes locked on hers, turned deadly serious. "Do I?''

"Yes. You really do.'' In his eyes, she saw acceptance and more—she saw faith in her. He believed in her. Joy filled her heart. He really believed in her.

"Yes," he said to the caller, then after a moment, he laughed. "Thanks for calling."

Knowing, Tessa beamed. "Good news."

Smiling, he kissed the tip of her nose. "You know it was. Ladyfair is pregnant. That was the vet. The second lab tests confirmed her pregnancy."

Tessa curled her arms around his waist. "So you got what you wanted."

"Not yet." He crushed her to him as if he'd never let her go. "Marry me."

Happiness filled her heart. More than anything else in the world, she wanted to say yes. "I do love you." She crumbled beneath her own words, tightened her arms on him. "But, Colby, marriage is—"

"What I want." He drew back to see her face. "You don't?"

She couldn't lie. She wanted it, a home, a family. Those were dreams of a lifetime. "Yes, I do. You know I do, but—"

Lightly he pressed fingertips to her lips to silence her. "Tessa, you can't say, 'yes, but,' when a man asks you to marry him. I believe in you. I will always believe in you. Whatever happens we'll deal with it."

"If we have children—"

His smile widened. "I like that idea." He chuckled. "And my mother would be thrilled."

She felt a lightness beginning to grab hold. "A

daughter would be like me, Colby.'' She thought he needed a reminder. ''She'll—''

''I know.'' He captured her eyes with his steadfast stare. ''She'll be just like her mother. Beautiful.'' He took her face in his hands.

Gently his mouth pressed down on hers. In the kiss was a promise that he'd be there for her—always. She hadn't thought she'd ever find love, find a man who'd accept everything about her.

''And special,'' he murmured against her mouth.

Tessa answered his long, lingering kiss. All she'd ever wanted was finally hers.

* * * * *

If you enjoyed Jennifer Mikels's Big Sky Cowboy, *you won't want to miss the exciting continuation of the popular series*

MONTANA

from Silhouette Special Edition—
Montana Lawman *by Allison Leigh*
is available in July 2003.

▼ SILHOUETTE®
SPECIAL EDITION™

AVAILABLE FROM 20TH JUNE 2003

BUT NOT FOR ME Annette Broadrick

Rachel Wood had never confessed her love to her boss, millionaire
Brad Phillips. So why, when she was in danger, did he insist on
whisking her to safety—as his convenient wife?

TWO LITTLE SECRETS Linda Randall Wisdom

After a fortnight in the arms of gorgeous Zachary Stone, Ginna
Walker sensed that he had a secret he wasn't ready to share. She was
sure that she could handle it...but she didn't know that he had *two*
little secrets...

MONTANA LAWMAN Allison Leigh

Montana

Librarian Molly Brewster had a new identity...and Deputy Sheriff Holt
Tanner had a case to solve. Would his search for the truth force her
into hiding—or would his love set her free and make her his?

NICK ALL NIGHT Cheryl St. John

Shock became passion when sexy single dad Nick Sinclair mistook
former neighbour Ryanne Whitaker for an intruder! Could his kisses
persuade her to swap city life for the warm glow of hearth and
home...forever?

MILLIONAIRE IN DISGUISE Jean Brashear

Tycoon Dominic Santorini introduced himself to Lexie only as Nikos—
but after an unplanned explosion of desire he couldn't help wondering
if she was really a corporate spy. Could he trust the truth he felt in her
every touch?

THE PREGNANT BRIDE Crystal Green

Kane's Crossing

Brooding tycoon Nick Cassidy married beautiful Meg Thornton when
he learned she was carrying his enemy's baby. The perfect plan for
revenge soon turned into love—but would Meg discover the truth?

SILHOUETTE
HOT SUMMER NIGHTS
Make this summer the hottest ever!
Dallas Schulze
Maggie Shayne
Lindsay McKenna

FREE

4 BOOKS
AND A SURPRISE GIFT!

We would like to take this opportunity to thank you for reading this Silhouette® book by offering you the chance to take FOUR more specially selected titles from the Special Edition™ series absolutely FREE! We're also making this offer to introduce you to the benefits of the Reader Service™—

- ★ FREE home delivery
- ★ FREE monthly Newsletter
- ★ FREE gifts and competitions
- ★ Exclusive Reader Service discount
- ★ Books available before they're in the shops

Accepting these FREE books and gift places you under no obligation to buy; you may cancel at any time, even after receiving your free shipment. Simply complete your details below and return the entire page to the address below. *You don't even need a stamp!*

YES! Please send me 4 free Special Edition books and a surprise gift. I understand that unless you hear from me, I will receive 6 superb new titles every month for just £2.90 each, postage and packing free. I am under no obligation to purchase any books and may cancel my subscription at any time. The free books and gift will be mine to keep in any case.

E3ZED

Ms/Mrs/Miss/Mr ....Initials..

BLOCK CAPITALS PLEASE

Surname..

Address..

....

....Postcode ....

Send this whole page to:
UK: FREEPOST CN81, Croydon, CR9 3WZ
EIRE: PO Box 4546, Kilcock, County Kildare (stamp required)

Offer valid in UK and Eire only and not available to current Reader Service subscribers to this series. We reserve the right to refuse an application and applicants must be aged 18 years or over. Only one application per household. Terms and prices subject to change without notice. Offer expires 30th September 2003. As a result of this application, you may receive offers from Harlequin Mills & Boon and other carefully selected companies. If you would prefer not to share in this opportunity please write to The Data Manager at the address above.

Silhouette® is a registered trademark used under licence.
Special Edition™ is being used as a trademark.